HONDO

HONDO

LOUIS L'AMOUR

BANTAM BOOKS
TORONTO · NEW YORK · LONDON · SYDNEY

HONDO

Bantam paperback edition/April 1983
Louis L'Amour Hardcover Collection/August 1983

Book designed by Renée Gelman.

If you would be interested in receiving bookends for The Louis
L'Amour Collection, please write to this address for information:

The Louis L'Amour Collection
Bantam Books
P.O. Box 958
Hicksville, NY 11802

ISBN 0-553-06245-X

Published simultaneously in the United States and Canada

Bantam Books are published by Bantam Books, Inc. Its
trademark, consisting of the words "Bantam Books" and the
portrayal of a rooster, is Registered in U.S. Patent and
Trademark Office and in other countries. Marca
Registrada. Bantam Books, Inc., 666 Fifth Avenue,
New York, New York 10103.

PRINTED IN THE UNITED STATES OF AMERICA

09876543

FOREWORD

W hat do we have here? The story of a lonely man hiding his loneliness behind a cloak of independence, a man as bleak as the land over which he rode, yet beneath the harshness and the necessary violence, a kind man, a just man, a man who had come to terms with the land in which he lived.

We have a woman, a woman with a home, no matter how thin the walls, how lonely the prospect. For her there were no ribbons and lace, no waltzes in the moonlight, no gossip over tea, no shopping in the store, only the sunrises and sunsets, a land of changing colors and cloud-shadows, long nights lying awake and alone when any sound might mean the end for her son and herself, but a woman with a home, a woman with a will to persist, to endure.

And we have an Apache leading his warriors in raids upon the white man, an Apache who respected courage and respected strength because they were qualities his people needed to survive. He was no poor, pathetic red man being put upon by whites, but a fierce warrior, a veteran of many battles, asking favors of no man. He did not fear the pony soldiers but welcomed them, for they brought into his harsh land the horses, the food, the clothing, and the weapons he could take from them. Often he admired the men he killed, often he was contemptuous of their ignorance and lack of skills.

Also, we have a boy, a boy who had a mother but needed a man to show him how to become a man himself. His own father was but a shadowy figure who came smelling of whiskey and the cheap perfume of other women, who came and went leaving no tracks that the boy could read, a boy who would build tomorrow, a boy who was the future.

I sing of arms and men, not of presidents, kings, generals, or passing explorers, but of those who survived their personal, lonely Alamos, men who drove the cattle, plowed the furrows, built their shelters against the wind, the men who built a nation.

I do not need to go to Thermopylae or the Plains of Marathon for heroism. I find it here on the frontier. I found it at Adobe Walls, at Beecher's Island, and in the aged Indian who charged the cavalry alone, with a worn-out knife. I found it in the Cheyenne warrior Mouse Road, whose enemies, when all his companions had been killed, drew off and told him he was too brave to kill, that he could go.

Mouse Road told them, "My brothers lie dead around me. How can I go back to my village and say they are dead, but I am alive? You must kill me, too." And three more enemies fell before he was killed.

Did Demosthenes or Cicero ever speak with greater eloquence than Chief Joseph when he said, "It is cold and we have no blankets. The little children are freezing to death. My people have run away to the hills and have no blankets, no food; no one knows where they are. I want time to look for my children and see how many of them I can find. Maybe I shall find them among the dead. Hear me, my chiefs. I am tired. My heart is sick and sad. From where the sun now stands I shall fight no more, forever."

These are the American stories, the stories I wish to tell, and if have not told them well, I shall have tried.

December, 1982

HONDO

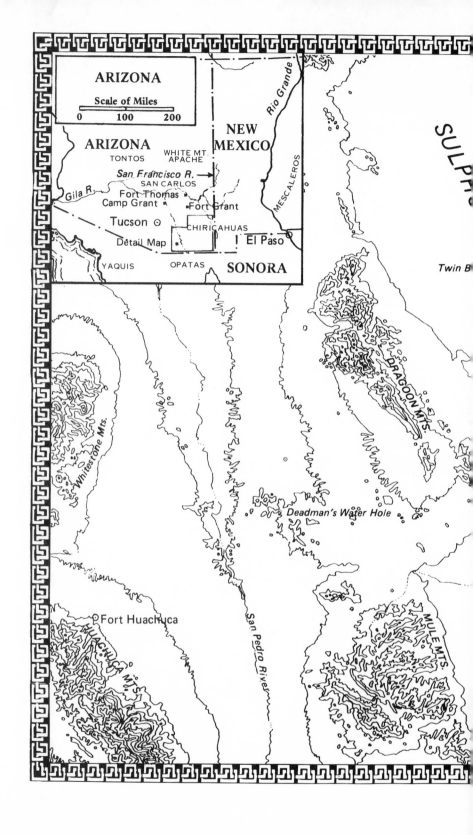

ARIZONA

Scale of Miles

0   100   200

ARIZONA

TONTOS

WHITE MT.
APACHE

San Francisco R.

SAN CARLOS

Fort Thomas

Camp Grant

Tucson ⊙

Detail Map

Gila R.

NEW
MEXICO

Rio Grande

MESCALEROS

Fort Grant

CHIRICAHUAS

El Paso

YAQUIS   OPATAS   SONORA

SULPH

Twin B

DRAGOON MTS.

Deadman's Water Hole

Whitestone Mts.

Fort Huachuca

HUACHUCA MTS.

San Pedro River

MULE MTS.

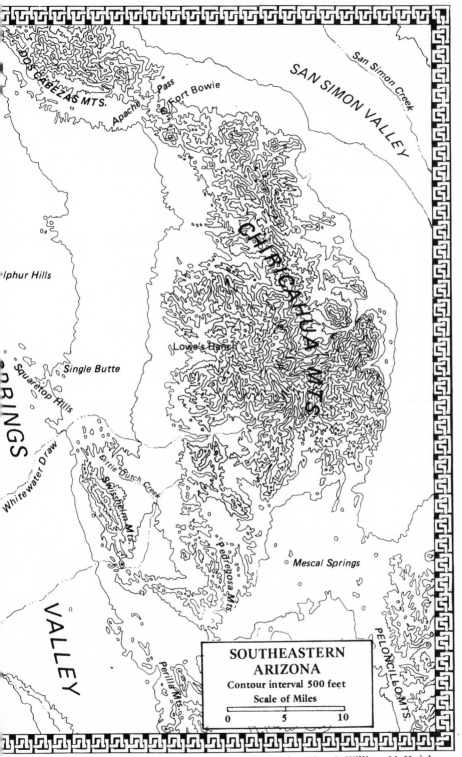

DOS CABEZAS MTS.

Pass

Apache

Fort Bowie

San Simon Creek

SAN SIMON VALLEY

Iphur Hills

CHIRICAHUA MTS.

Lowe's Ranch

Single Butte

Squaretop Hills

RINGS

Whitewater Draw

Little Dutch Creek

Swisshelm Mts.

Pedregosa Mts.

Mescal Springs

PELONCILLO MTS.

VALLEY

Perilla Mts.

**SOUTHEASTERN
ARIZONA**
Contour interval 500 feet
Scale of Miles
0   5   10

Map by Alan & William McKnight

ONE

H e rolled the cigarette in his lips, liking the taste of the tobacco, squinting his eyes against the sun glare. His buckskin shirt, seasoned by sun, rain, and sweat, smelled stale and old. His jeans had long since faded to a neutral color that lost itself against the desert.

He was a big man, wide-shouldered, with the lean, hard-boned face of the desert rider. There was no softness in him. His toughness was ingrained and deep, without cruelty, yet quick, hard, and dangerous. Whatever wells of gentleness might lie within him were guarded and deep.

An hour passed and there was no more dust, so he knew he was in trouble. He had drawn up short of the crest where his eyes could just see over the ridge, his horse crowded against a dark clump of juniper where he was invisible to any eye not in the immediate vicinity.

The day was still and hot. Sweat trickled down his cheeks and down his body under the shirt. Dust meant a dust devil or riders . . . and this had been no dust devil.

The dust had shown itself, continued briefly, then vanished, and that meant that he also had been seen.

If they were white men fearful of attack, they were now

1

holed up in some arroyo. If they were Apaches, they would be trying to close in.

He studied the terrain with care, a searching study that began in the far distance and worked nearer and nearer, missing no rock, no clump of brush, no upthrust ledge. He saw no further dust, heard no sound, detected no movement.

He did not move. Patience at such a time was more than a virtue, it was the price of survival. Often the first to move was the first to die.

Hondo Lane took out the makings and built another cigarette. When he struck the match he held it well back in the foliage of the juniper, keeping the flare invisible. He drew deep on the cigarette, returning his attention to the terrain.

The rough-looking mongrel dog that followed him had lowered himself into the soft earth beneath another juniper a dozen yards away. The dog was a big brute, gaunt from running.

It was hot. A few lost, cotton-ball bunches of cloud drifted in a brassy sky, leaving rare islands of shadow upon the desert's face.

Nothing moved. It was a far, lost land, a land of beige-gray silences and distance where the eye reached out farther and farther to lose itself finally against the sky, and where the only movement was the lazy swing of a remote buzzard.

His eyes wandered along the ridge. To his right there was a shallow saddle, the logical place to cross a ridge to avoid being skylined. Logical, but obvious. It was the place an Apache would watch.

There were junipers beyond the ridge, and broken boulders upon the ridge itself. In less than a minute he could cross the ridge and be in the shelter of those junipers, and if he took his time and made no sudden moves to attract the eye, he might easily cross the ridge without being seen.

He thought none of this. Rather it was something he knew, something born of years in wild country.

Hondo Lane crossed the ridge into the junipers and hesitated briefly, studying the country. His every instinct told him those riders had been Apaches and that they were somewhere close by. Yet the dog had given no sign.

He eased his weight in the saddle and checked the eagerness of the horse, which smelled the water in the river not far ahead.

Finishing his cigarette, he pinched it out and dropped it to the sand and angled down the slope. He slid his Winchester from its scabbard and rode with it across the saddle, keeping his horse to a walk. Vittoro was off the reservation with his fighting men, and that could mean anything. Council fires burned and there was much coming and going among the lodges. Mescaleros had been hunting with the Mimbreños and the border country was alive with rumors.

Hondo Lane could smell trouble, and he knew it was coming, for others and for himself.

Ahead lay the river, and after the rains it would be running full and part of the crossing would be swimming. Lane liked no part of it. Since the rains he had crossed the trails of four bands of Apaches and they had been riding without their women and children, which meant raiding. Young bucks out to lift some hair or steal horses.

He went down the slope to the river, knowing there was no way of avoiding the crossing. He used every bit of cover and changed direction frequently, heading toward an inviting sand bar that led far out into the stream, yet when he was near it he suddenly switched direction and rode behind a clump of cottonwood and willow, going into the water in the shadow of the trees, and quietly, to make no splash.

The dog went along with him and together they crossed. As the buckskin went up the bank, Hondo heard the twang of a bowstring and felt the buckskin bunch its muscles under the impact of the arrow. As the horse started to fall, Hondo Lane rolled free.

He hit the sand on his shoulder and rolled swiftly behind a drift log. When he stopped rolling he was looking past the butt end of the log with his rifle in position. He saw a movement of brown and his finger tightened and the rifle leaped in his hands. He heard the *whop* of the striking bullet and saw the Apache roll over, eyes wide to the sun.

As he fired, he moved, getting into a new position in coarse grass with almost no cover. And then he waited.

Hondo dried his sweaty palms on his shirt front and blinked to keep the sweat out of his eyes. The sand was hot beneath him, the sun hot upon his back. He smelled the stale sweat of his body, the smells of tobacco, horse, and greasewood smoke that lived with him. He waited, and there was no sound.

A fly lighted on the back of his hand, he heard the sound of water running over stones. Around him were the gray bones of a long dead tree. His shoulder cramped.

There was no movement; only a small bird started to land in a clump of brush, then veered away. It was a small bunch of brush and Hondo took a chance. He fired suddenly into the brush, spacing his shots. He heard a faint, gasping cry and fired again at the same spot.

Rolling back to his former position, he waited, then looked past the butt of the log. He saw a moccasin toe dig spasmodically into the sand, then he saw it slowly relax.

Two Indians, or more? He lay still, ears alert to sound. The moccasin toe remained as it was. A tiny lizard appeared on a branch near him and stared, wide-eyed. Its tiny heart pounded, its mouth gaped wide with heat. He dried a palm, then flicked a stone into the brush twenty feet away. He heard it fall, and no sound followed.

Probably not more than two. His mouth felt dry and he dearly wanted a drink. Yet he waited, wanting to take no chance, and knowing too well the patience of the Apache.

Only after several minutes did he ease away from the log and circle to get a better look. The Apache lay still, his lower back bathed in blood that glistened redly in the hot afternoon sun.

Hondo Lane got to his feet and moved closer. The bullet had struck the Indian in the chest. It had cut through his body from the top of his chest and had come out in the small of his back, breaking his spine.

Lowering the butt of his rifle, Hondo took off his hat and

mopped his brow with a handkerchief. He looked again at the sprawled brown body of the Indian, then glanced over at the other. Both are dead . . . and this was not a good place to be.

The dog stopped under a tree and lowered himself to the ground, watching him. Hondo glanced at his dead horse, then stripped it of saddle, bridle, and saddlebags. It was a load, but swinging them together, he shouldered them and started off through the trees, walking with a steady stride. The dog rose from the ground in one easy movement and started after him.

Reaching the stream at a bend, Hondo Lane walked into the water on an angle that pointed upstream. When he was knee-deep he turned and walked back downstream and stayed with the stream for half a mile, then emerged and kept to rocks along the stream for some distance farther, leaving them finally at a rock ledge. When he left the rock he was again walking upstream. He used every device to hide his trail, changing directions with the skill of an Apache, and finally he reached a ridge, which he followed, just below the crest.

The sun sank and the long shadows crept out from the hills, but Hondo Lane did not rest. He moved on, checking distance by the stars, and continuing along the ridge. When he had walked two hours into the night, he finally lowered his heavy burden to the ground and rubbed his shoulder.

He had come to a halt in a tiny circle of rocks among scattered piñons. The rocks rimmed a cup that sat down at least ten feet lower than the hills around. Unrolling his blankets beneath a tree, he made a quick supper of a piece of hardtack and jerked beef. Then he rolled in his blanket and slept.

At dawn he was awake. He did not awaken gradually, but his eyes opened quickly to consciousness and he listened, then glanced at the dog. It lay some yards away, head resting on paws. Hondo relaxed and swiftly rolled his blankets. After a quick check from the edge of the cup, studying the country, he returned and gathered dry branches from the curl-leaf, a shrub whose branches give off a hot flame and are almost smokeless.

He built a small fire under a piñon so what little smoke there was would be diffused by rising through the branches. He made coffee, ate more jerky and hardtack, then eliminated all evidence of his fire and brushed leaves and sand over the spot. Carefully he removed evidence of his resting place and tracks. Then, shouldering his saddle and saddlebags again, he left the cup and started along the ridge.

The morning air was fresh and cool. He walked with a steady stride, rarely pausing to rest. His lean, wolf-hard body, baked by too many suns and dried by winds, carried no soft flesh to melt away under the sun. At midmorning he heard birds chirping and went toward the sound. A shallow basin in the rock held water. He dropped to his belly and drank, then moved back, and the dog moved in, lapping the water gratefully, but with eyes wary.

Among the rocks near the water Hondo Lane smoked a cigarette and studied the country. There was no movement but an occasional buzzard. Once he saw a lone coyote. He drank again, then shouldered his saddle and moved on.

Once he stopped abruptly. He had found the old track of a shod horse. The track was days old, and from its appearance had been made before the rain. Little was left but the indentations. Thoughtfully he studied the terrain around him. It was an extremely unlikely place for a rider to be. No soldier would be in such a place unless scouting for a larger command.

Shouldering his burden once more, Hondo backtrailed the hoof marks, finding two more tracks, then losing them on lower ground where the rain had washed them out. Finally, making a guess, he quartered on his route and cut across the shallow valley, moving toward a place of vantage from which he could see the country.

He saw a bunch of squaw cabbage and broke off a few stalks and walked on, eating them as he went. Twice more he found isolated tracks of that same shod horse, and then suddenly the dog stiffened.

Hondo eased himself back to the ground. There was sparse grass where he lay, a few scattered chunks of rock. He lowered his saddle among the rocks and lay perfectly still. The dog, a few yards away, lay absolutely immobile. He growled, low and deep.

"Sam!" Hondo's whisper was quick, commanding. The growl subsided.

Several minutes he lay still, and then he heard the movement. There were nine Apaches, riding in a loose bunch, heading in a direction roughly parallel to his own. He lay still, avoiding looking directly at them for fear of attracting their attention.

Nine. At this distance he wouldn't have a chance. He might get three or four before they hit him, and then that would be all. Nor was there any shelter here. Only his absolute immobility and the neutral color of his clothing kept him from being seen.

He listened to their movement. They did not talk. He heard the rustle of the horses through the coarse growth, an occasional click of hoof on stone. And then they were gone.

He lay still for several minutes, then got up and cut across their trail, still occupied with those shod hoof tracks. They had all been made at the same time. This meant a white rider had spent some time in the area. He might still be here. One horse could mean another.

A few miles farther and suddenly the cliff broke sharply off and he was looking into a deep basin at the bottom of which lay a small ranch. It was green, lovely, and peaceful, and with a sigh he started down the slope, walking more slowly.

Below him, near the worn poles of the corral, a small boy was playing. Suddenly, attracted by some sound, he lifted his head and looked up the slope at the descending man.

"Mommy! Mommy!"

A woman came to the door of the cabin, shading her eyes against the sun. Then she walked out to the child and spoke to him, and together they watched the man on the hillside. He walked still more slowly, the fatigue of the long days and his heavy burden at last catching up with even his iron strength. She hesitated, then turned quickly and walked back to the cabin.

Hanging in a holster from a peg on the cabin wall was a huge Walker Colt. She lifted the heavy weapon from its holster and walked back to the door, placing it under a dish towel on the table where it would be immediately available.

She put her hand on the child's head. "You let Mommy do the talking," she said quietly. "Remember!"

"Yes, Mommy."

Hondo reached the bottom of the slope and walked slowly toward the cabin. As he drew near his eyes went from the house to the corrals and the open-face shed that sheltered an anvil, a forge, and a few tools. His eyes went beyond, searching, still wary. Not even the presence of the woman and child in the doorway dispelled his suspicion.

"Remember," the woman whispered, "no talking."

Hondo lowered his saddle to the ground under the shed and took off his hat as they walked toward him. He mopped his face. "Morning, ma'am. Howdy, son."

"Good morning. You look like you've had trouble."

"Yep. I lost my horse while I was gettin' away from Indians a few days ago. Made a dry camp above Lano last night." He gestured toward the dog. "Then Sam here smelled Apaches, so I thought I'd make some more miles."

"But why? We're at peace with the Apaches. We have a treaty."

Hondo ignored her comment, looking around at the stables. There were several horses in the corral. "Yes, ma'am, and now I've got to get me a new horse—borrow or buy one. I'll pay you in United States scrip. I'm ridin' dispatch for General Crook. My name's Lane."

"I'm Mrs. Lowe. Angie Lowe."

"Can you sell or hire me a horse, Mrs. Lowe?"

"Of course. But I've only got the plow horses and two that are only half broken. The cowboy that was training them for me got hurt and had to go to town."

They walked toward the corral together. Two of the horses were obviously mustangs, wild and unruly. Hondo Lane moved around, studying them carefully. Both were good animals.

"I'm sorry my husband isn't here to help you. He's up in the hills working some cattle. He *would* pick this day to be away when we have a visitor."

"I'd enjoy meetin' him, ma'am." He glanced toward the boy, who was walking toward Sam. "I wouldn't pet that dog, son. He doesn't take to petting. And now, ma'am, if you'll allow me, I'll give those horses a try."

"Of course. And I'll get you some food. I imagine you're hungry."

Lane grinned. "Thank you. I could eat."

Lane hesitated before going to the corral. There was work that needed to be done around here. The little things that are done by a man constantly living around were undone. The recent rains had run off the barn and started to run back under the foundation timbers, gouging out a hole. Another rain and that hole would be much larger. It should be filled and the water trenched away toward the arroyo.

He rolled a smoke and lighted it, then leaned on the corral bars. The two mustangs moved warily, edging away from the man smell and the strangeness. Both had good lines and showed evidences of speed and power. There was a lineback that he liked, a dusky, powerful horse, still wearing his shaggy winter coat.

Lane went through the bars and into the corral, rope in hand, cigarette dangling from the corner of his mouth. The horses moved away from him, circling against the far side of the small corral. He watched them moving, liking the action of the lineback, and studying the movements of both horses.

He talked quietly to the horses and dropped his cigarette into the dust. He was conscious that the boy was perched on the corral, watching with excitement. Dust arose from the corral, and he shook out a loop. The lineback dun tossed his head and rolled his eyes, moving away from the threat of the loop.

Hondo smiled, liking the horse's spirit. He spoke softly, then moved in. When he made his throw it was quick, easy, and deft. The loop dropped surely over the bronc's head, and the horse stopped nervously. He knew the feel of a rope, at least. That much he had learned, even if he had not learned the meaning of a saddle.

Leading him to the corral bars, Hondo talked softly to him, stroking his neck and flanks. The mustang shied nervously, then began to quiet down. Finally he nosed at Hondo curiously, but shied when Hondo reached for his nose.

Making no quick movements, Hondo walked to the bars and crawled through. When he had his saddle and bridle he walked back, dropped them near the horse, talked to him a little, and then after rubbing his hand over the dun's back he put the saddle blanket on him. Then the saddle. The horse fought the bit a little, but accepted it finally.

Once, glancing toward the house, he saw Angie Lowe watching from the doorway.

Leaving the saddle and bridle on the horse so the animal could get used to them, Hondo left the corral. He stood beside the boy, letting his eyes trace the line of the hills. It was amazing to find this woman and her child here, in Apache country.

Suddenly curious, he walked toward the stable, then circled around the bank of the stream and back to the house. The only horse tracks entering or leaving since the rain were his own. Thoughtfully he studied the hills again, and, turning, walked back to the house.

There was a tin washbasin on a bench beside the door, a clean towel and a bar of homemade soap beside it. Removing his hat and shirt, he washed, then combed his hair. Donning the shirt again, he stepped inside.

"Smells mighty good, ma'am," he said, glancing at the stove. "Man gets tired of his own fixin'."

"I'm sorry my husband picked today to go hunting those lost calves. He would have enjoyed having a man to talk to. We welcome company."

Lane pulled back a chair and sat down opposite the plate and cup. "Must be right lonely here. Specially for a woman."

"Oh, I don't mind. I was raised here."

Sam came up to the door and hesitated, then came inside, moving warily. After a minute he lay down, but he kept his attention on Hondo. He seemed somehow remote and dangerous. There was nothing about the dog to inspire affection, except, perhaps, his very singleness of purpose. There was a curious affinity between man and dog. Both were untamed, both were creatures born and bred to fight, honed and tempered fine by hot winds and long desert stretches, untrusting, dangerous, yet good companions in a hard land.

"What can I feed your dog?"

"Nothin', thanks. He makes out by himself. He can outrun any rabbit in the territory."

"Oh, it's no trouble at all." She turned back to the stove and picked up a dish, looking around for scraps.

"If you don't mind, ma'am, I'd rather you didn't feed him."

Curiously she looked around. The more she saw of this man, the more she was impressed by his strangeness. Yet oddly enough, she felt safer with him here. And he was unlike anyone she had ever known, even in this country of strange and dangerous men.

Even when he moved there was a quality of difference about him. Always casually, always lazily, and yet with a conservation of movement and a watchfulness that belied his easy manner. She had the feeling that he was a man that lived in continual expectation of trouble, never reaching for it, yet always and forever prepared. Her eyes dropped to the worn holster and the polished butt of the Colt. Both had seen service, and the service of wear and use, not merely of years.

"Oh, I think I understand. You don't want him to get in the habit of taking food from anyone but you. Well, I'll just fix it and you can hand it to him."

"No, ma'am. I don't feed him either."

When her eyes showed their doubt, he said, "Sam's independent. He doesn't need anybody. I want him to stay that way. It's a good way."

He helped himself to another piece of meat, to more potatoes and gravy.

"But everyone needs someone."

"Yes, ma'am." Hondo continued eating. "Too bad, isn't it?"

She moved back to the stove and added a stick of wood. She was puzzled by him, yet there was a curious attraction, too. Was it simply that he was a man? That the woman in her needed his presence here? That the place had been needing a man too long?

She stirred up the fire, turned over a charred stick, and moved back to the table. He ate slowly and quietly, not talking, yet without the heedlessness of manner of so many Western men, accustomed as they were to living in camps and bunkhouses and away from the nearness of women.

His boots were worn and scuffed. And there was a place on his left thigh where the jeans had been polished by the chafing of some object. A place that might have been made by a holster. Only this man wore his gun on his right side. Had he, then, worn two guns? It was unlikely. Not many men did.

"You're a good cook, ma'am." Hondo pushed back from the table and got to his feet.

"Thank you." She was pleased, and showed it. She smoothed her one good apron with her hands.

"A woman should be a good cook."

He walked to the door and hesitated there, looking out over the yard, then at the trees, the arroyo, and finally the hills. As he did this he stood just within the door, partly concealed from the outside by the doorjamb. Then he put on his hat, and turning he said, "I'm a good cook myself."

TWO

It was hot and still in the afternoon sun. The boy perched on the corral bars and watched Hondo Lane lead the lineback dun through the gate, then replace the bars. From the lean-to he got a sack of grain and put it across the saddle. The dun humped his back and sidled nervously away, but when Hondo walked off, leading him, he hesitated only briefly, then followed along.

The mustang was used to rope, and had probably been saddled before, but not often. Angie Lowe had said that he had never been ridden, and there was little time to waste. Hondo walked around the yard a few times, then removed the grain sack and proceeded to take off and put back the saddle several times.

He glanced at the boy. "Gets him used to it," he said. "He'll learn it's nothin' to be scared of. First thing they've got to know: not to be scared. After that, if they find out the man in the saddle is boss, then they'll do to ride."

He talked to the horse a bit, then stripped off the saddle and bridle, returning him to the corral. As he did so, Hondo stepped back and looked around at the hills, a slow, studying glance.

13

Angie Lowe came from the house and the boy trotted away and began picking sticks from under the cottonwoods, where a few dried twigs and branches lay.

"It surprises me that you picked the most savage horse," Angie commented. "He's always been a fighter."

"Wouldn't give a plugged nickel for one wouldn't fight. Horse without spunk will let you down when the going's tough."

He glanced toward the woodpile and then at the boy, starting toward the house with an armful of kindling.

"Only fair I should trade kindling for a meal." He picked up the ax and placed a chunk of wood against a log, in position for splitting. Then he glanced at the ax. It had no edge. Obviously it had not been sharpened in some time. It was equally obvious that it had suffered much misuse.

"No edge," he said. "I'll turn the grindstone if you'll hold the ax, Mrs. Lowe."

"I'll be glad to. That ax has been driving me crazy."

The grindstone was a heavy, old-fashioned type and turned heavily. He started the stone turning and the rasping whine of steel against stone cut into the clear, still air of the afternoon. He paused in the turning and poured water in the funnel-shaped can that allowed slow drops to fall on the turning stone. "You were raised here on the ranch, Mrs. Lowe?"

"Yes, I was born here. My husband was raised here on the ranch, too."

He glanced at her, starting the wheel turning again. Watching her intent eyes as she moved the ax against the turning stone, he found himself liking the stillness of her face. She was, he suddenly realized, a beautiful woman. Even the hardness of desert wind and sun had not taken the beauty from her skin. But there was a shadowing worry around her eyes that disturbed him.

It made no sense, a woman living like this. Not this woman, anyway. Maybe she had been born to it, maybe she was doing a better job here than almost any woman could be expected to do. It still was not right.

He straightened from the wheel and glanced around briefly

at the hills, then bent to the turning again. The woman was skillful with the sharpening ax, he had to admit that.

When he straightened again she returned to the subject of her husband. "He was an orphan. His parents died in a wagon-train massacre. My father took him in and raised him here."

"Handy," he said.

The wheel turned again and the ax showed an edge, carefully honed down now.

He straightened, taking the ax from her hands. She looked at him, not understanding his use of the word. She said as much.

"Figures are against it. Only young fellow in a thousand square miles, only young girl in a thousand square miles, and they get in a whirl about each other. That's what I mean. Handy."

"I guess it was a coincidence. But they say the right two people are going to meet by an arrangement of destiny."

He held the ax in his hands. He looked at her thoughtfully. "You believe that, Mrs. Lowe?"

"Yes, I do."

He studied her for a minute, and she met his eyes frankly, a little puzzled, and faintly excited. He turned away. "Interesting," he said.

He walked slowly to the woodpile. There were several logs and a number of large trimmed branches. There were also some stumps that had been grubbed out, and some chunks of ironwood. These last were all their name implied, hard as iron, but they burned with a bright and beautiful flame.

His first swing of the ax split the chunk he had chosen. Methodically he went to work, and for a few minutes she stood watching him. There was a beautiful and easy rhythm in his movements. He handled his body as if it were all one beauti-fully oiled and coordinated machine. Nor was he awkward on his feet, as are so many riding men. He moved, she thought, like an Indian.

He did not look up, moving easily from stick to stick. He cut through the log, then cut through it again, handling the ax with the skill of long use. Several times he paused, each time his eyes circled the hills rimming the basin.

Keeping clear of the ax, the boy gathered the big chips into a neat pile, watching as Hondo swung the blade. Sinking it into a log for the last time, Hondo straightened. "Son, always sink the blade into a log when you've finished cutting wood. The edge stays clean of rust."

Angie walked from the house, watching him repile the wood to keep too much of it from becoming rain-soaked at any one time. As he piled it, the boy looked toward Sam, who watched from close by.

The child hesitated, looked longingly toward the dog, then at Hondo. "Pet?"

"You do what you want to, young one."

Hesitantly the boy reached his hand toward the dog. Sam bristled, then snapped. The boy drew back quickly, frightened and half ready to cry.

Angrily Angie turned on Hondo. "Really, Mr. Lane, if you knew the dog bites, why would you—"

"Mrs. Lowe," Hondo said patiently, "I told the boy earlier not to touch the dog, but still he wanted to pet him. People learn by gettin' bit. The youngster learned."

To cover her confusion, she turned sharply on the boy. "Johnny, don't ever touch that dog again!"

Johnny looked up at Hondo, and Hondo grinned, dropping a hand to the child's head. "Don't let it get you, old-timer. You'll get snapped at a lot in this life. Might as well get used to it. Don't trust nothin' too much."

He wiped his hands on his shirt front. "And now I'll get back to that horse."

The lineback had been thinking it over. He was losing his fear of the saddle and bridle, for already he had discovered they did him no harm, but he did not like the bit, and he did not like being led around. Yet he had learned the folly of fighting a strangling noose.

He stood quietly, trembling a little, as Lane came down the rope toward him. He submitted to being tied, and although he jerked his head back several times, he finally took the bit. He worked it in his jaws, not liking it. He jumped a little and tightened when the blanket was thrown over his back, and then the saddle.

Later he would learn to blow himself up against the girth, but that he had not discovered as yet. He felt it tightened and tensed again. The man's voice was soothing, and he was so sure of himself that the horse almost unconsciously relaxed. Then he was led outside and the man gathered the reins.

Angie, half frightened, had come to the door to watch. Johnny clutched her hand, wide-eyed and excited. Hondo Lane stepped into the saddle.

Instantly the horse bunched his muscles and bucked. The man remained in the saddle. Angrily the dun tried to get his head down so he could really go to bucking, but the man in the saddle kept his head up. Then suddenly the reins slacked a little and the lineback began to pitch. He buck-jumped across the yard, swapped ends swiftly, and tried to throw himself over backward. Yet the man stayed with him.

There was a certain brutal beauty in the struggle between man and horse. The mustang, given his chance, decided to make a fight for it. Infuriated by the thing clinging to his back, the powerful horse bucked wildly, but the man remained in the saddle. Seeming to anticipate the horse's every move, he swayed and bobbed with the maddened plunging of the horse, but stuck to the saddle and even seemed to urge the lineback on to do his worst.

And the lineback liked a fight. He put his heart and his powerful muscles into the battle, and with it all the fiendish ingenuity he had acquired in his years on the range and inherited from his bronco ancestors. It was a good battle.

Dust arose, lather flew from the plunging horse, but Hondo Lane stayed in the saddle, and suddenly the horse lunged into a run. He raced down the trail, went under a low branch, and tried to charge into the brush, but Lane was ready for him and swung him into the trail and they went up and over the hill with no obvious slackening of pace.

Behind them the dust settled. The yard was empty of turmoil, the trail dust settled, the skyline of the hill remained empty. Angie waited while the slow minutes passed. Johnny tugged at her hand. "Mommy, will he come back? Will the man come back?"

"Yes, Johnny," she replied quietly. "He'll come back. I'm sure of it."

Yet as the slow minutes dragged by, she began to wonder if he might be lying up there with a broken leg, or if the horse was still pounding off into the desert on that furious run. She watched the skyline, and the skyline was empty.

Nervously she bit her lip, then shaded her eyes to look again, circling the hills as she had seen him do, and as she often did herself.

For the first time she found it impossible to understand her own feelings. There was an element of strangeness about the visitor that disturbed her, but was it only that? Was it his strangeness? Was it the fact that she had been so long alone? Or was there something else?

He kept her excited and upset as she had never been around any man. Why should that be? Moreover, and what was far worse, she was sure he knew how she felt. Yet he did not look like a man who would have seen much of women. He was remote, and—the woman in her told her this—he was lonely.

Yet he was a man who shielded his loneliness as he did all his feelings. He was ruthless, as ruthless with himself as he would be with others. Oddly, despite his strangeness, she felt more at home with him than she ever had with anyone else. When he had as much as called her a liar she had not been offended.

The horizon was still empty. She walked back inside and glanced in the mirror, straightening her hair. Her heart was beating strangely, and it was no way for a married woman to feel, no way for any respectable woman to feel.

That might be it . . . that might be the thing that disturbed her so. He made her feel like a woman. He made her feel . . .

yes, that was it. She blushed into the mirror. He made her feel like a female.

She turned quickly away from the glass, a little shocked at herself. That was no way to be thinking. He would be back soon, and she must not even allow such thoughts to enter her mind.

When he came back over the hill the dun was lathered but moving smartly. Lane glanced at the woman in the door and was surprised by the relief in her eyes. Had she been worried about him or the horse?

And this was a lot of horse. The dun had fight. He also had speed and bottom. Lane had not allowed him to run himself out, just enough to let the horse know that the rider could handle that, too. Then he circled and rode back to the ranch.

A lot of horse, all right. Hondo Lane glanced up at the door and at the woman standing there. And that was a lot of woman, too. Slim, but graceful and with a lot of spirit and heart.

"Ready to shoe now, ma'am. And while I'm at it, I'll shoe that pair of plow horses of yours. Their hoofs are clean grown over the front plate."

"Thank you very much. They do need shoeing, I guess."

He led the dun to the stable, stripped off bridle and saddle, and he took a handful of hay and gave the mustang a brisk rubdown. It was new treatment for the horse and he took it nervously, needing time to decide whether he liked it. But again the calm sureness of the man prevailed. There was simply nothing the dun could do about it. He was wary to kick, but he got no chance with this man, who seemed to understand just how he felt.

Lane stoked the forge and heated the shoe. Angie watched, impressed. "You'll find everything there." Then she turned to Johnny, who stood watching with excited attention. "You'd better go to the house and get ready for your nap."

Johnny was hurt. "Oh, Mommy, can't I stay?"

"You'll do as you're told!" Her voice was firm. "Run along now."

With a backward glance, Johnny trudged off toward the

house, hating to leave the glowing forge and the ringing hammer, hating also to leave this man who treated him so matter-of-factly, almost as if he were a man himself.

Angie Lowe looked at Hondo's face from time to time, uncertain as to the best words. There was a point she wanted to get across to him, but everything she could think of to say seemed somehow flat and foolish.

Finally, shading her eyes toward the hills, she said, "I don't see any dust coming down from above. I guess my husband's having a hard time finding those strayed calves. Perhaps he won't be home until late tonight."

Lane made no comment, continuing with his work. She watched him, noting the deft, sure movements and the easy way he had with the horse. He seemed almost not to have heard her.

"He might even camp out in the hills and come in tomorrow after you're gone. He'll be so sorry to have missed one of our very occasional visitors."

She looked at his face, but there was no indication of feeling or hint of what he was thinking. Suddenly she was confused and wanted only to get away.

She drew her hands down over her apron. "I'd better go look after Johnny."

"Mrs. Lowe?"

His tone stopped her as she turned away, and, half frightened, she looked around at him. He was turning a shoe in the forge, not looking at her. She noted the breadth of his shoulders and the narrow hips. He must be awfully strong.

"You're a liar," he said.

His voice was so calm, so matter of fact that it was impossible to take offense.

"An almighty poor liar," he added.

"I don't understand." She faced him, drawing herself up a little, a picture of dignity and reserve.

There was, he thought, a good deal of queenliness about her at such moments. She had breeding, that was obvious. Not even this ranch and the simple clothing could deprive her of that. It was like seeing a thoroughbred horse in his winter coat. The blood lines were there, despite season or situation.

He nodded toward the horses in the corral. "Those horses haven't been shod in months. Your ax hasn't had an edge on it in just as long, and no man has been using it. The five-pound tea can in your house is empty. Your husband's been gone a long time."

Angie Lowe's face was pale. "Now, see here, Mr. Lane, I don't think you have any right to—"

"Not talking about rights. I'm talking about lies. Why'd you lie to me, Mrs. Lowe? You were scared that you wouldn't be safe with me here and your husband away. That it?"

"That's part of it."

Hondo took the shoe to the anvil and hammered it out. The sparks flew and the ring of the hammer precluded any conversation.

"Women always think every man that comes along wants 'em."

She turned swiftly, chin high, and walked toward the cabin. Her heart was pounding and she had difficulty breathing.

"Besides," she heard him say, "I looked around when I first came. Nobody has been out of here ahorseback since the rain. Maybe not for a long time before."

When he had finished shoeing his own horse, he turned it back into the corral and led out the plow horses. It was growing late but he trimmed down their hoofs and went to work with the shoeing.

He stopped when he had finished with the first of the big horses and rolled a smoke. He stepped away from the stable and inspected the rim of the valley again.

This was a nice little place. The right man could do a lot with it. Of course, it was no place for a woman to be alone, and no right kind of man would ever leave such a woman alone in this country . . . unless he was dead.

He read more into the place than she would have believed. There had been a lot of work done here, good solid work that a man could be proud of, and it had been done by a man with pride in the work. But that had been a long time ago.

Since then the place had been slowly running into the ground, and here and there were the fixings of a man who was shiftless, a rawhider if he ever saw one.

Her father must have built the cabin. It was carefully done by a man who knew his business. It was built of stone, and the stones were fitted carefully. It was logically located both for use and for defense and for shelter from northers. A good man with a rifle could stand off almost any attack from this place, situated as it was.

And the corrals had been well built. They needed work now. The whole place needed work. The roof of the shed needed thatching. The water hole should be cleaned out, too. And once there had been a small dam to catch water in a pool to irrigate a small kitchen garden. The dam had been washed out by some cloudburst and never repaired.

A man could look around and draw his own conclusions. Her father had died, and her husband, whoever he was, had let the place run down. She had been trying to keep it up, but it was a man's job, and she had her woman's work and that child. He was a well-behaved child, and you could always tell what the parents were by the child.

She was a woman, all right. Scarcely more than a girl in years, but all woman. And mighty pretty. He took the cigarette from his lips and looked at it, took one more drag, and dropped it to the earth, where he automatically rubbed it out with his toe. He'd best get on with his shoeing. It was growing late. It was sundown, and in this cup it would grow dark sooner than it would up there on the level country. If you could call it level.

He heard the door close and saw her coming, carrying a water pail. He did not turn or speak as she walked by behind him, but heard her footsteps hesitate a little as if she had thought to speak, then went on. Returning, she stopped and shifted her pail to the other hand.

"Mr. Lane?"

"Yes, ma'am?"

"You're right. I was lying. My husband is overdue. In fact, he should have been home long ago."

Hondo nodded. "Figure Apaches killed him?"

She stiffened, shocked at his acceptance of the idea that had occurred to her many times. "Of course not. There are a hundred possible explanations."

She knew of several that she never allowed herself to consider. She had known Ed Lowe enough to understand him.

"Indians are one of them."

"But we're at peace with the Apaches, except for a few renegades who—"

"Mrs. Lowe." Hondo straightened from his job. "If you've got good sense you'll pack up you and that child and come out with me. There's a lot of trouble cookin' in the Apache lodges. The main chief, Vittoro, has called a council. A full report of it is in the dispatches I'm carryin'."

"Oh, no." She shook her head with decision. "We've always got along splendidly with the Apaches. They drink and water their horses at our spring. I haven't seen the great Vittoro, but there've been plenty of Apaches here."

"I've seen Vittoro." Hondo's tone was grim. "Before the treaty. He had forty scalps hung in his horse's mane."

"But that was before the treaty."

"We broke that treaty," Hondo persisted patiently. "There's no word in the Apache language for 'lie,' and they've been lied to. If they rise there won't be a live white in the territory."

Angie was not convinced. "They wouldn't bother me. Us, I mean. We've always got along well."

Hondo returned to his work. There was little to do now, and he was tired. The hammer drove home the nails, straight and sure. She watched him, noting the way the horses trusted him. Even that wild mustang he had broken had seemed to trust him. And there was Sam, that curious dog. She looked at Hondo's face, wondering what was behind it.

What was he thinking? What, above all, did he think of *her*? Woman-like, she wanted to know. What kind of man was he? What had his home been like? What sort of woman would he want? A queer little shock of something almost like fear went through her. Suppose he was married?

Well, then. Suppose he was? It was no business of hers. What could it possibly matter? Nevertheless, the thought disturbed her, and she looked at him keenly, trying to find the marks of a woman on him, but she could find none. But you could not tell with his sort. A woman made her impression, but it was inside of the man. A woman could change a weak man, but not such a man as this. Yet to be loved by him would be . . . would be . . .

"People I know," Hondo commented on her last remark, "man and wife, got along real well for twenty years. Then she blew a hole in him a stagecoach could drive through. She got mad. The Apaches are mad."

"I have nothing to worry about, I'm sure."

"Nice to be sure."

Sam trotted up as they were talking. The big dog had been away on some business of his own. From the tuft of fur at the corner of his jaw, the business had concerned rabbits. He seated himself several yards away and watched Hondo. Both were somehow remote, untouchable, unreachable. She studied the dog as if hoping to learn more of the man.

"That's a strange dog you have."

"I don't have him."

She was puzzled. "But the two of you are together!"

"He stays with me. He can smell an Indian at half a mile."

He returned the last of the horses to the corral and racked up the old shoes on the corral fence. He looked at Angie as he spoke, and, fighting the desire to look away, she met his eyes.

"He smells Indians? I don't believe it."

"Lots of dogs smell Indians. You can teach them."

"Teach them? How?"

He leaned on the rail, shoving his hat back from his brow. The hair curled damply against his forehead. She repressed an urge to reach up and push it back.

The sun was down but it was still light, and the air was turning cool with the desert night. Long streaks of red re-

mained in the sky, and on the western edge of a cloud there
was a blush of old rose. Pale yellow light lingered on the
topmost leaves of the cottonwoods, and their leaves whispered
in the dry way they have.

Shadows gathered beneath the trees and beneath the western shoulder of the mountain, reaching out in long fingers
toward the cabin and toward the man and woman who stood by
the corral, talking.

"You get a puppy and hire a tame Indian. Then cut a willow
switch and four or five times a day you have the Indian beat
the puppy with the switch, and all the rest of his life he'll signal
when he smells an Indian."

"Beat a puppy?" She was shocked. "How cruel!"

He shrugged. "That's the way you do it."

"And anyway," she scoffed, "I don't believe a dog can smell
Indians. I mean as different from anyone else. You or me, for
instance."

He gathered the tools and returned them to the bench
beneath the lean-to. "They can, Mrs. Lowe. Matter of fact,
Indians can smell white people."

"I don't believe that."

He smiled, and the smile lightened his features with a whim-
sical, almost boyish expression. "It's true, ma'am. I'm part
Indian, and I can smell you if I'm downwind of you."

She was uneasy, but to cover it, she laughed, then shook her
head. "Why, that's impossible!"

"No, Mrs. Lowe. It's not impossible."

He stepped around so that he was facing her and downwind
of her. She felt a strange tenseness come over her, and fought
it, with sudden desperation. He stood close, his nostrils widening, narrowing. For a moment she thought he was going to . . .

"You baked this morning." His voice was matter of fact. "I
can smell fresh bread on you. Sometime today you cooked salt
pork. I can smell that on you. And I can smell soap all over
you. You took a bath. On top of that, you smell all over like a
woman. A woman's got a different smell from a man. Not salty

and sharp, but kinda soft and rich and warm. I could find you in the dark, Mrs. Lowe, and I'm only *part* Indian."

He was standing close to her and they were both aware of a sudden tension. She started to speak but would not trust her voice. There was something about him. . . . It was impossible. It was ridiculous, but there it was.

She drew back a little. She smoothed her apron. "I think I'll go back to the cabin," she said hastily.

She turned swiftly, fighting down an overwhelming urge to run, to escape to the familiar surroundings of her own house. To get away somewhere, anywhere, away from him, away from this feeling.

It was wrong. It was all wrong. She should not feel like this about any man.

She told herself it was wicked, but deep within her she did not believe it.

And what sort of man was he? What did she know about him? What could she know? He had said nothing of himself, just nothing at all.

There was something big and hard and sure about him, something in the way he moved, or something from inside of him.

She had the feeling that there was nothing anywhere that could frighten or disturb him. That he was a man who knew himself, knew his strength and his weakness, who had measured himself against the hard land of his living, against the men of that land, and against its wilderness. Whatever he had discovered, he was no longer afraid.

It was dark now, and the wind stirred among the leaves and moaned softly around the roof. She knew that sound. It was a lonely sound, a sound that always frightened her, because it made her know her aloneness. But not tonight. Tonight even the wind had a comforting sound. And why was that?

She avoided the thought, turning swiftly to work, busying herself with preparations for supper, trying not to think of that big, easy moving man out there in the gathering dusk.

She had known other men. There had been many visitors to

the ranch while her father was alive, and some of them had courted her, yet none of them had ever disturbed her as she was now disturbed.

He was moving around out there. She could hear the murmur of his voice, talking to the horses. She heard the twang of a pitchfork prong striking some object. He was feeding the horses. Soon he would be through. Her throat felt tight. Soon he would be coming to the house.

She heard his footsteps on the hard-baked earth. He was coming now. He was coming to the house. She looked blankly around, biting her lower lip as if she had forgotten something. He was coming to the house, and it was night, it was dark. . . .

THREE

S he put her hand to her hair, looked around, and went to the door as she heard him stop. There was a moment of silence, then a knock.

Angie put out her hand to the door, then took it quickly away. "What do you want?"

"I've fed and grained your horses."

"Thank you."

"I'll bed somewhere near till morning."

She heard him turn away. She hesitated, then she opened the door. He stopped and turned, clearly revealed in the light from the doorway.

"You can't sleep outside. There's a wind rising. I'll fix a pallet for you in the corner."

Hondo hitched his saddle higher on his hip and followed her into the house. Behind him Sam slipped through the door and sat down near it, looking at the room with bright, interested eyes.

Angie turned up the kerosene lamp and Hondo took in the room with a glance. Her bed and Johnny's were in a small alcove, curtained by an Indian blanket. He removed his hat and hung it on a peg, then dropped his saddle in a corner out of the way.

She took blankets from an old trunk and carried them to a corner. She indicated a buffalo robe to him and he spread it on the floor, then covered it with the blankets. She started to bring a pillow, but he shook his head.

"Never use a pillow. Only sometimes my saddle. Too soft. A man can't hear good with a pillow around his ears."

"But you'll be asleep."

"Yes, ma'am, but I wake up easy. This country a man had better."

She straightened the blankets with a few quick, feminine, and totally unnecessary movements, then straightened. Without looking at him, she explained, "It would be uncivilized to let anyone sleep outside. And after all, we are civilized, aren't we?"

"Speaking for you, of course. Speaking for me?" He considered it for a minute, then agreed. "I guess you could call me that."

"I have to set some batter for morning. I hope the noise won't bother you."

"It won't." He sat down on his pallet and pulled off his boots. "Good night, Mrs. Lowe."

He drew his pistol from its holster and with the gun in his hand he rolled over on the pallet and pulled a blanket around him. Almost at once his breathing was even and regular. Glancing at him, Angie saw that he was actually asleep.

He must be very tired. How far had he walked that morning? It had been just past daylight when he lost his horse, and it had been a long, very hot day. Yet he moved little in his sleep, and she worked, only dimly conscious of his presence. It had been a long time since there had been a man in the house, and it was a comforting thing.

As she mixed the batter her thoughts returned to Ed. Where was he? Had he been killed by the Apaches? No, he was simply gone, and he might not come back at all. Nor could she wish for him to come back, for these past few months they had grown further and further apart, and he had worked less and less. Most of the time he was gone, finding some excuse to be away in town.

He gambled, she knew that, and returned home only when he was broke. What had seemed to be love she realized now had been merely the natural result of proximity. It was not so amazing a coincidence as Lane had made it seem, for there were no other girls around, and few men. They had been together, and it had been a natural thing for them to talk of marriage. And Ed Lowe had got along well with her father.

In fact, he usually got along well with people when it was to his advantage. He had deliberately set himself to cultivate her father, for in those days the ranch looked good, and it was growing. After her father died, Ed came to realize that a ranch grows only by the work that is put into it, and he gradually let it go, selling a few cattle, breaking wild horses for the Army, and sometimes, she suspected, stealing them from the Indians whenever he could.

She had tried. Not even Ed Lowe could deny that. She had tried hard, because she was his wife and because he was Johnny's father. But it had not worked, and now he had gone off and it had been a long time since she had seen him. Now, considering the matter, she knew she hoped he would not come back.

He wanted no responsibility. The chores of the ranch nagged at him and irritated him, and the problem of buying cattle and tending them on the range was not for him. Her father had got along well with the Indians. Even old Vittoro knew him, and they had done business together. Several times he had given the Apaches sugar and tobacco, always sure they understood that it was as a gift to friends and not tribute.

There was none of this feeling in Ed Lowe. He despised the Apaches, and feared them.

She put the pan aside and went to the lamp to turn it down. As she did so her eyes fell upon a brass plate set in the cantle of his saddle. She bent closer, suddenly curious.

FIRST PRIZE
Bronc Riding
Hondo Lane

She drew back quickly, startled by the name. Her sudden movement caused a stirrup to fall to the floor, and Hondo Lane was on his feet in one swift movement, gun in hand.

With almost the same movement, she had dropped back to where she had put the Walker Colt earlier. Instantly she lifted it. "You're *Hondo* Lane! The gunman!"

"I carry a gun."

Slowly the muzzle of his gun lowered and he blinked in the light.

"Only last year you killed three men in a gun fight. We heard about it. *Three men!*"

"Yes, ma'am."

He smiled and stepped toward her, reaching for the gun, and in a panic of some sudden emotion, she knew not what, her finger shut down on the trigger. The hammer fell with an empty click and he stood with the muzzle of the gun against his chest, looking down at her.

Frightened by what she had done, she stood helpless while he gently took the gun from her hand. "Shouldn't point a gun at anybody when there's an empty chamber under the firing pin. It can be seen mighty plain. Specially with the light behind it."

He armed the Colt, then dropped it in the empty holster.

"I keep it that way because of Johnny."

"Keep it out of reach, and with a load in the chamber."

He ran his fingers through his hair. "Empty gun's no use to anybody, ma'am. If you need that, you'll need it fast."

"I might have shot you."

"Yes, ma'am."

He turned toward his pallet. "Guess I sort of scared you. Usual noises don't bother me. It's those unusual ones that wake a man. Sorry, ma'am."

He sat down on the pallet and once more he rolled over and

drew up the blanket. He was once more asleep. He still held the gun.

Lane . . . Somehow the thought of his being Hondo Lane had not entered her mind. She should have realized who he was, for she had heard he had become a dispatch rider and scout for General Crook.

Crook valued such men, and made every effort to recruit them. She had seen the General when he first arrived on the Arizona station. He had not been in uniform. In fact, he rarely was, and he was traveling without fuss or ceremony. She had heard it said that no man alive knew more about pack trains than General Crook, and he got on well with the Apaches.

She stretched out in her bed, tired but wakeful. She had almost shot Hondo Lane. She had not intended to. So why had it happened? What had she been afraid of? She felt her face grow warm in the darkness and she turned her back on the room, trying to forget his even breathing. Yet she could not forget. And it was a friendly, comforting sound. For the first time in months she slept without fear, without worry.

Outside the wind moaned around the eaves and the cotton-wood leaves rustled with their dry, companionable whispering.

She awakened once during the night and lay awake for several minutes. She had been worried about fuel, and now she need no longer worry. And the horses were shod. He had accomplished so much in so little time, and cutting through the big log . . . It would have taken her days.

If she had to leave, the payment for the horse would help. But she could not think of leaving. This was her home, and here she could eke out a living whether Ed returned or not. She could shoot, and she had been able to kill an occasional rabbit or antelope. Johnny was getting older and in a few more years he could take over the hunting and she would at least have the land to leave him. And she could trade with the Indians.

Shortly before daylight Hondo awakened quickly. He sat up, listening, placing the sounds of the predawn hour. Then he got to his feet and slung on his gun belt, dropping the Colt into its holster.

From the window he scanned the ranch yard. There was a faint gray-yellow light in the east. The yard was empty and still. The horses were standing relaxed and lazy. Returning to his pallet, he folded the blankets, then the buffalo robe and placed them in a neat pile upon a chair.

With a glance at the curtained alcove he picked up his hat and boots and eased open the door, stepping out into the brisk chill of morning. Lowering himself to the step, he put on his hat, then his boots.

The horses came to meet him and he forked hay for them. The lineback let his hand touch it before it shied away, and then he went to the creek.

The water gurgled darkly over the stones with little places of bubbling water where it ran around a branch or other obstruction. He removed his hat and, squatting, bathed his face in the cold water. The creek water was miraculously soft and very cold. He bathed his eyes, spluttering a little, and then combed his hair and straightened away from the creek.

The trees were dark and mysterious, and the cold of the morning was bracing and good. A few stars lingered, reluctant to abandon the clear sky to the coming sun. He took his time, skirting around the ranch, looking for fresh tracks, finding none but those of deer that had come down to graze on the greener grass around the edges of the corral.

The garden her father had irrigated was growing, but the few rows were painfully small, and obviously irrigated by hand now. Across the creek he saw a clump of squaw cabbage and there were no broken stalks. He must tell her about it, for apparently she knew nothing of the desert plants on which the Indians survived.

There was food in the desert if a man knew where to find it, and the Apaches knew. That was the item that defeated the Army. The Apaches lived off the country they passed through, and they knew all the water holes, and could if necessary go for several days without water, just carrying a pebble in their mouths. But the Apaches knew the plants that conserved water too.

Hondo rolled a smoke and glanced around the rim of the hills as his tongue touched the paper. Of course, the food the Apaches loved was mule meat—and that meant Army mules. An Apache preferred it to any other, with horse meat second, and only after that would he consider beef or mutton. Pork he would not eat at all.

Yet there was plenty to eat in the desert if a man knew where to look. Lane crossed the stream and gathered a double handful of squaw cabbage. He was walking back toward the house when the door opened and Angie Lowe stepped out.

"Squaw cabbage," he said. "Lots of it across the creek. Mighty good stew when you boil it with meat. Some folks like it raw."

She accepted the whitish stalks and put them down on the table inside. "Breadroot out there, too," he said, "an' you can grind mesquite beans into flour an' bake them into a loaf."

"You must have learned a lot from the Indians."

"Some," he said. "They've lived here a long time."

He walked on to the corral and roped the lineback. When he led it out of the corral he bridled and saddled it, then went to the house for his saddlebags and rifle.

"You're leaving?"

"Yes, ma'am. Got to go on." His eyes met hers. "Sure you won't come along?"

"No. This is all I have."

"Dam ought to be rebuilt," he said. "Hard to get water in the garden."

"If you're going, I ought to wake Johnny to say good-by to you."

"Was it me," Lane coiled his rope, "I'd let him sleep. Youngsters grow sleeping. But you do what you want to."

"He's delighted with the whistle you gave him. It's more like a flute than a whistle."

Lane felt uncomfortable. He liked to avoid good-bys, and

this was leading to one. He fiddled with the girth, rearranged the saddlebags.

"Learned to make them when I lived with the Mescaleros. My squaw used to make them for all the youngsters in the camp."

"You lived with the Apaches?"

"Five years."

She hesitated, but her curiosity overcame her reluctance to pry. "You had an Indian wife?"

"Wife . . . squaw. Took the liberty of borrowing a few feet of rope off that roll in the lean-to. Mine was 'most worn out. I'll be glad to pay you for it if you'll let me."

"Of course not."

He tied the rope to the corral post, then to the pommel of the saddle, and moved the horse back to stretch the newness out of the rope. She fidgeted wanting to know more but hesitant to ask. There was no sound from the house. The air was still fresh and cool but carried the promise of a hot day. As he worked, she watched him, reluctant to see him go.

"It must have been interesting, living with the Apaches."

"I liked it."

"This Indian wife you have—"

"Had. She's dead." He spoke quietly, without emotion.

"I'm sorry. I didn't mean to bring up an unhappy memory."

He turned, letting the horse stand. He pushed his hat back on his head and considered her remark. "I don't remember anything unhappy about Destarte."

"Destarte! How musical! What does it mean?"

"You can't say it except in Mescalero. It means Morning, but that isn't what it means, either. Indian words are more than just that. They also mean the feel and the sound of the name. It means like Crack of Dawn, the first bronze light that makes the buttes stand out against the gray desert. It means the first sound you hear of a brook curling over some rocks—some trout jumping and a beaver crooning. It means the sound a stallion makes when he whistles at some mares just as the first puff of wind kicks up at daybreak.

"It means like you get up in the first light and you and her go out of the wickiup, where it smells smoky and private and just you and her, and kind of safe with just the two of you there, and you stand outside and smell the first bite of the wind coming down from the high divide and promising the first snowfall. Well, you just can't say what it means in English. Anyway, that was her name. Destarte."

Rather amazed, Angie stared at him. "Why, that's poetry!"

"Huh? Didn't mean to go gabbing." He looked around at Angie. "You remind me of her. Some."

He untied the rope and began to coil it again without looking at Angie. "Good rope," he commented. "Sure I can't pay you for it?"

"I remind you of an Indian girl? Was she fair?"

He turned and looked at her without emotion. He inspected her hair, her coloring and her face. She flushed as his eyes went over her figure.

"Her hair was black as ten feet down. It shined black like those plums you find up on the Powder. You know how the wing of a crow is shiny? Black and gleaming." He tied the rope to the saddle horn. "That's the way her hair shined." He tightened the knot. "I'd like to pay you for this rope. Dispatch riding I've got the right to give you United States Army scrip."

"You loved her?"

He hesitated thinking about it his eyes wandering toward the hills. He hitched his belt a little and took out the makings. "I don't know. I needed her."

"But if she was dark and I'm fair?"

"Why you remind me?"

"Yes."

"I dunno. It's hard to figure. I thought about it. You walk like her with your head up."

He put the cigarette in his lips. "You walk like an Indian. You don't toe out like a white woman."

He looked at her and their eyes met. He took the cigarette from his lips and took the front of her dress in his left hand and drew her to him and their lips met. There was nothing forceful about it, and she neither resisted nor helped, yet she was far from merely acquiescent. And when they parted her face was a little pale. She stepped back, not frightened, but not sure of what it meant.

"I'm surprised at you, Mr. Lane."

"No, you're not surprised, Mrs. Lowe. You knew."

"I'm a married woman."

"I thought about that, too. I thought about it a long time. Last night."

She touched her lips with the back of her hand and took another step back. Nothing about it had seemed wrong. It had seemed natural, right. Angie was puzzled at her own feelings and trying to find a meaning for them.

"Maybe I kissed you because you make me think of Destarte. Or maybe because I hate to think of your hair drying, slung from the center pole of an Apache wickiup. But a long time ago I made me a rule: I let people do what they want to do.

"I got it figured now. Handsome woman like you, walks with her head up, ought to kiss a man before she dies."

"You're very strange, Mr. Lane."

He swung into the saddle and the lineback humped its back, then settled down, restless, but aware of the man in the saddle and remembering the fight of yesterday. "I don't know about that," he said thoughtfully. Then he looked away. "Good-by Mrs. Lowe."

She waited standing very still in the center of the yard until he went over the hill, and even then she did not move, but stood there, silent and alone in the middle of the bare yard. The dust settled into the trail and the rim of the hills showed nothing but the morning sky, brightening. It would be very hot.

She turned, picked up her pail and walked to the spring.

FOUR

N o man knows the hour of his ending, nor can he choose the place or the manner of his going. To each it is given to die proudly, to die well, and this is, indeed, the final measure of the man.

The forty-seven men in Company C rode with an awareness of death, for there were no recruits in their twin files. All were seasoned, desert-wise fighting men who knew the character and ability of their enemy.

The mission allotted to Company C was a wide sweep of the basin to warn, and to bring to the camp if possible, all ranchers, prospectors, trappers, and pioneer homebuilders who might still be at large and unaware of the impending outbreak of fresh hostilities. Their commanding officer was Lieutenant Creyton C. Davis.

At thirty-two, Creyton Davis was a case-hardened veteran. Graduated from the Point in time to serve the last year of the War between the States, he had transferred west following the war in time to ride with Carpenter to the relief of Forsyth at Beacher's Island. Later he was at the destruction of Tall Bull's villages in '69.

In the five succeeding years he had campaigned in the

desert, working from a series of bleak, wind-swept sun-baked posts against the Apaches, that fiercest and wiliest of guerrilla fighters.

Squinting his eyes against the sun glare, he tried to penetrate the shimmering heat waves. Beyond the heat waves were the mountains, and from the liquid movement before them arose the sentinel spires of the saguaro, those weird exclamation points of the desert.

No sound disturbed the fading afternoon, no sound but the creak of saddle leather, the rattle of accouterments, the click of hoofs on stone—and these were always with them.

Sweat trickled through the dust on his face, and alkali had made his uniform stiff and gray. His neck itched from the heat and dust, and his skin was raw from the baking sun. Nowhere, in all that vast expanse, was there movement. Yet out there somewhere was the Apache.

When he saw the solitary rider sitting motionless against the background of the hill, he almost drew rein.

Cotton Lyndon was a square-built man of forty, his face so seamed and lined with desert years that he looked twenty years older. The nickname was born of his hair, once corn yellow, now pure white, and his one apparent vanity.

He swung his horse alongside the Lieutenant's. He indicated the direction in which they rode. "Water yonder."

"What do you think?"

"They're around. I don't know where."

"See anything of Lane?"

"Won't—not until he wants you to."

"The General expects him. He's overdue."

Lyndon tilted his hat against the sun. "He'll make out." There was a slight change in his voice. "Hope you an' me do as well."

Davis glanced aside at Lyndon, a quick frown shadowing his eyes. Coming from Lyndon, it sounded ominous. Davis knew enough of such men to realize they often knew things without being able to explain why they knew them. It was, he supposed, a result of some subconscious perception.

As if in answer to his thoughts, Lyndon added, "That's Vittoro out there."

Davis let his horse walk on a dozen steps, then turned in his saddle. "Sergeant Breen? There's water ahead. We'll make camp."

Breen involuntarily glanced at the sun. Two good hours of riding left, and Davis was not a man to waste time on a trail.

"We may not find more water and I want the men to rest," Davis said. "A bad day tomorrow."

He felt an immediate satisfaction with the spot. The water was a small stream, clear and cold, that flowed from the mouth of an arroyo scarcely fifty yards deep. At the head of the arroyo the spring flowed down from a dozen cracks in the rock.

The spot selected for the camp was in a basin under shelving rock, and about twenty yards out from the face the ground sloped away, offering a fine field of fire. The camp was masked from the wide plain by a ridge of volcanic rock several hundred yards off.

It was a sudden relief from the saddle and the men relaxed quickly, getting their horses out and mounting guard at once. Old Pete Britton, who had just joined as a scout, went atop the cliff for a look around. There was little talking, the men bathing, filling canteens, and taking the unexpected rest.

The sun declined, the shadows reached out from the cliff, faint smoke lifted from the few fires. Lieutenant Davis walked alone to the edge of the hill and with his glass studied the volcanic ridge, then the plain. He saw nothing.

He had the feeling now himself. Despite that, there was a solid confidence within him. If they had to face serious trouble, he could not face it with a better company of men. Sergeant Breen had a record of twenty years of service, and he had been in the Southwest when Mangus Colorado was active, and Cochise. After that he had seen service at Bull Run, Shiloh, and the Wilderness.

Corporal Owen Patton had ridden with Nathan Bedford Forrest, and had been a lieutenant himself. He was a tall, rangy young man with blond hair that waved back from his brow. He was the best shot in the company, and one of the finest horsemen. O'Brien had been a freighter before he joined up, veteran of many Indian battles. Silvers and Shoemaker had been buffalo hunters.

The faint, smoky haze of evening lay over the desert, and the clouds were tinged with the rose of the setting sun. Davis stopped by the spring, drank of the cold water, then walked back to where his bedroll was dumped against the cliff's face. He threw his campaign hat aside and sat down, digging writing materials from his saddlebags.

Lyndon opened his eyes and watched him. It was the first time he had ever seen Davis writing on patrol. Sergeant Breen noticed it, too, and looked quickly at Lyndon. No courier was being sent back. The command would return in just two days . . . if it returned.

Breen checked the guards and added a word of warning, then returned to camp. Lyndon was lighting his pipe.

"Too quiet out there," Lyndon said. "I wish Pete would get back."

"Comin' now."

Pete Britton had lived fifty hard years, forty of them in Indian country. He did not stop, nor did he look toward Lyndon and Breen, but walked on by to where Davis sat.

Davis glanced up. "Yes?"

"No use to ride by the MacLaughlins'."

Davis felt something inside him go sick and empty. He had liked the MacLaughlins, had sat at meals with them more than a dozen times. Three stalwart men and two women, four youngsters.

"You sure?"

Pete Britton's irritation sounded in his reply. "Sure? Ah'm almighty sure." He jerked his head to the north. "Smoke. Too much for a small fire. That barn an' house, most like, sometime this afternoon."

Lieutenant Creyton C. Davis sat very still, the trial of command before him. If he moved out now, one or more might still be alive. He might effect a rescue. On the other hand, he would be riding off into darkness with tired men against a relentless and ruthless enemy that would know he was coming. And if they were gone, the tracks could not be followed before daybreak.

If he led out his command and men were lost, he would be asked why. If he did not lead them out and some of the family could be saved, he would also be asked why. He sat very still, then said quickly, "Thanks, Pete. Anything more you can tell me?"

Pete Britton shook his head. "Daylight, mebbe."

The old man turned and walked away to join Breen and Lyndon, who had listened. Britton jerked his head. "Ain't no fool. Afeerd he'd want to go traipsin' after them in the dark."

Breen shook out his bed and pulled off his boots. He sat for a minute, looking off toward the first faint stars, then he rolled in his blankets. When he finally dropped off to sleep he could still hear the faint scratching of the Lieutenant's pen.

In the first clear light of dawn Davis stood over the campfire with a cup of coffee. He glanced around for Britton.

"Pulled out before sunup," Lyndon said.

Horses were led out and saddled and mounted, and the company moved out. Dust lifted, sun glinted on rifles. Davis swung his horse into the trail toward the MacLaughlins'.

Lieutenant Davis did not doubt that Britton had been correct, but it was his duty to check, and to bury the bodies if they were to be found. It was, he reflected, no pleasant task for such an early morning.

With a lift of his hand, Cotton Lyndon moved out to the flank and angled up the slope. Davis watched him, frowning slightly then turned in his saddle. "Sergeant?"

"Yes sir?"

"We're riding into trouble. I don't know where it will come from or when. Pass the word along. No lounging in the saddle, no carelessness. I want every man alert. This is no routine patrol."

Breen dropped back, and Davis let his eyes go again to Lyndon. The man was riding quietly, keeping his mount to the crest of the ridge and in such a position that he could see over without exposing more than his hat and eyes.

Dust climbed, the sun grew warm. Through a notch in the trees Davis saw a fleck of bright green. That would be the cottonwoods at the MacLaughlin ranch.

As they came out of the draw into the wide valley, all was still in the morning sun. Where the ranch house had stood they could see blackened ruins and a slow lift of smoke. Davis tightened his lips. His eyes swung around the valley.

"Sergeant?"

When Breen moved up, he said quickly, "As we move in I want a perimeter defense. Detail a burial party. There'll be bodies down there. Have Corporal Patton take six men and sweep those woods."

"You think they're still here, sir?" Breen was dubious. "It ain't like them, sir."

"They're Apaches, Breen."

"Yes, sir. Of course, sir."

Breen dropped back. The Lieutenant was right, of course. There was no telling what an Apache might do, except that it would be the most unexpected thing. Breen had heard it said that Davis was too careful. With Apaches a man could not be too careful.

The company moved into the ranch yard and swung down. The bodies were there. After a quick glance, Lieutenant Davis turned aside. MacLaughlin, his two sons, and the women. They had all died here. It was better than being prisoners, except, perhaps, for the children. The Apache, a cruel and vicious fighter, was kind to children, often adopted them into the tribes and treated them gently. With women it was otherwise.

He glanced around. Patton was moving out with six men toward the small grove of trees, the burial party was working, other men had moved out, and the perimeter defense was set up. Suddenly Davis glanced around. There was no sign of Lyndon.

Anxiously he walked to the edge of the yard and glanced around the hills. No rider, no dust.

Breen walked toward him, hat in hand, mopping his face. "Nasty job sir. They're hacked up mighty bad."

"How many do you think?"

"Maybe a dozen. Not more'n twenty." Breen put on his hat. "Nothing we could have done, sir. It was earlier than Britton thought. Yesterday morning, I reckon." He indicated the corral. "Horses didn't eat all the hay they were fed."

Davis nodded. It fitted with what he himself had observed. The Indians must have been waiting out there at daybreak, lying perfectly still, probably scattered around the ranch.

MacLaughlin had died at the corral, struck down by three arrows. Jim MacLaughlin, the older of the boys, had evidently received some warning, for he had rushed to the door, gun in hand. There was a spot of blood at the barn that could mean a dead or wounded Indian. And Alex MacLaughlin lay sprawled and dead with an overturned bucket beside him.

"Must've been comin' from the spring," Sergeant Breen said, "an' he saw something and yelled. Then they got him. Jim rushed to the door, an' he stood 'em off a spell. One of the women had her hands blackened like she'd been firin' that old muzzle-loader."

Davis tightened his lips. Corporal Patton stopped before him and saluted sharply. "Woods clear, sir. Found where several Indians had bedded down, sir. Looks like they'd remained some time."

The burial party was returning, their faces gray and sick.

"All right, Sergeant. Mount up."

They were in their saddles and moving out when they saw the rider. A horse was coming down toward them at a dead run and on the back was the bobbing figure of a man. It was Cotton Lyndon.

But it was such a Cotton Lyndon as they had never seen. The proud white mane of hair was stained red with blood. Strips had been peeled from his hide. Blood streamed from his wounds and stained the sides of the paint pony on which he was tied.

Patton raced out and caught up the horse and men surrounded the dying man. For an instant, as his body was lowered to the ground, Lyndon's eyes rolled up to Davis.

"Vittoro. Must have seventy . . . men." Lyndon caught at Davis' sleeve. "Get out! Get out, Davis, while you can!" He choked, but clung with agonized grip to the sleeve. "Stalkin' you! Mescaleros, Mimbreños, Chiricahaus, an' Tontos . . . all up! More comin'! Get to . . . fort."

The scout's body sagged back to the grass. Lieutenant Davis straightened. "All right, Sergeant. Bury him here, where he lies."

He swung back into the saddle. No sign of Pete Britton. No sign of an Indian. And he had not met Hondo Lane.

Lane was out there somewhere, and his dispatches were important. His thoughts leaped ahead, placing the few outlying homes. The decision was his, and it might mean life or death for the poor unwarned devils who were at their ranches or in camp. It might also mean the end to his command.

He glanced around at them, his face expressionless. He knew every man of the company. Knew something of their troubles, trials, and tribulations. Clanahan, who drank too much, Nabors, who was surly and hard to get along with, and Sandoval, who wore a knife scar he had picked up from a *señorita* in Tucson.

They moved on into the desert and the morning. Lieutenant Creyton C. Davis rode beside the guidon now. His eyes reached out to the hills, and he thought of Vittoro.

Cunning as a wolf, the old chief was a fierce and vindictive fighter. His treatment of Lyndon had been a warning of what he intended for them all, if they were caught alive. And how had he caught Lyndon alive? Cotton Lyndon, who knew so well all the Apache tricks? And where was old Pete?

The command moved on, trotting now, and swung around a group of low hills. They passed another burned-out ranch, and buried the dead. Davis hesitated, then made his decision. "Sergeant, have the men refill their canteens here. We'll swing south toward Mescal Springs. When we reach the open country we'll dismount and walk the horses."

"Dismount?"

"Yes Sergeant." Davis hesitated, then said quietly, "We're going back, Sergeant. These ranches are answer enough. There's no reason to go on. If anyone is alive up ahead, they know more about the Indians than we do." He paused. "We'll dismount in the open country where they can't ambush us. That will rest the horses. We'll make camp early, as we did last night. When the men have rested we'll mount up and move out slowly. I dislike to leave a good fight, but if the tribes are out, the General should be informed.

"Moreover," he smiled, "we may get a chance to trap the old boy himself. He's waiting for something, you can bank on that. For more warriors, possibly. I think he's waiting to get us in rougher country, where he can use an ambush. If he thinks we'll go on south of Mescal, he'll probably wait. There isn't better ambush country in the world."

Breen nodded, waiting. Lieutenant Davis had always let him know just what he was thinking. There was nothing of the martinet in the man and he believed that if the men knew the score, each could carry on in better fashion.

"Once he knows we've started back, we'll have a fight."

"Does the Lieutenant hope to lead him back?"

Davis hesitated. "If we can, Sergeant. If we can."

The plain opened before them, and once they were well into it, he slowed the column and dismounted the men to save their horses. Apparently they were moving into rugged country where by tomorrow every mile would offer a new trap. Would Vittoro wait? Or would he attack at the first opportunity?

Vittoro might be waiting for a contingent of Apaches from another tribe. A successful battle and much loot would do much to cement the allegiance of his allies. Nobody would realize this better than Vittoro.

They walked slowly. It was very hot. Dust arose. A road runner darted away ahead of them, a streak of dull brown against the desert. A rattler buzzed from under a mesquite bush. They walked on.

A mile, three miles. The hills were dawning nearer now. No sign of Pete Britton.

The Lieutenant mounted the column and they moved out at a walk, and they came up to Mescal Springs at four in the afternoon. Under double guards, they bedded down for a rest.

The sun dropped behind the hills, long shadows reached out, the mesquite clumps turned to blobs of blackness against the gray of the desert. Horses had been rubbed down and watered, a few fires were lighted, coffee was made.

Against the boulder where he sat, Lieutenant Davis waited. He was a slender young man with a face darkened by desert suns, a pleasant face, composed and still now.

He signaled Breen and Patton. They drew near and then dropped to their knees as he motioned to them. "We'll move out at midnight," he told them, "keeping downslope in the sand. If we get away, when we're a mile out we'll mount up. Then we'll move at a trot."

When they had gone, he turned to his blankets and stretched out. He would not sleep, he knew. He might rest a little. . . .

A hand was shaking him. It was Breen. "Time, Lieutenant. Midnight."

Davis sat up, amazed. He had slept for hours. Quickly he was on his feet, straightening his uniform, checking his gun. His horse was saddled and waiting.

All was dark and silent. Taking the lead, he moved out. The slope was soft sand and stoneless, as was much of the valley bottom. The small column moved without sound.

For ten minutes they walked. Corporal Patton moved up from the rear. "Seems quiet, sir."

"All right." He turned. "Sergeant, pass the word along. Mount up. Walk the horses another ten minutes."

After ten minutes he lifted the column into a trot. Holding the pace, they held on down the valley. If they had escaped the Indians, there would be no following them until morning. It would give them a safe lead. He was already thinking ahead, checking over the country in his mind, and he knew the place.

It was not a good place for an ambush, hence was sure to be

unexpected by Vittoro. There was a place among low hills. . . .
He rode on, heading directly for the fort, yet his plan was
made. It was a chance to trap Vittoro and he meant to take it.
The defeat of the Apache war chief might easily end the outbreak. Certainly it would end the trouble for a time. Until
another chief was selected.

He held the horses to a trot for an hour, then slowed to a
walk. All night they moved steadily, taking only two short
breaks. At daybreak the country was opening out and by noon
they would be less than forty miles from the post.

Suddenly he saw the hills. It would be here. . . . He halted
the column and quickly gave his orders. On the spot, the
situation looked even better than he had remembered.

The valley down which they had been riding had ended,
leaving them in a country of rolling hills. Two low hills lay on
each side of the meadow, and he rode down this meadow, then
moved to the right and concealed his horses in a draw. On the
far slope of the hill there were several hollows ideal for
concealment.

"Corporal," Davis looked at Patton, "take Silvers and Shoemaker and get behind that hill opposite. When the enemy are
well into the meadow, fire on them. I want three Indians down
with those three first shots. Then fire again, get into your
saddles, and swing wide and get back here. Understand?"

"Yes, sir." Patton hesitated. "You're going to be here, sir?"

Davis nodded. "When you fire, I think they'll run to this hill
for shelter."

"Yes, sir."

Silence fell, the little dust settled. The sun rose well into the
sky, the earth smelled faintly. A few flies buzzed. An hour
passed slowly. Men drank from their filled canteens. They
waited.

Clanahan saw them first. Davis felt his scalp tighten. They
had been strengthened. There were more than seventy. There
were ninety or more.

No matter.

They seemed to have no fear, no realization of what lay

ahead. They rode steadily down the meadow. Two Indians were well ahead, and suddenly one of them drew up sharply. Instantly Davis knew the man had seen the bent grass where the horses had turned. The Indian wheeled his pony and yelled sharply.

From across the meadow there was a crash of shots. The Indian fell headfirst off his racing pony and turned head over heels in the grass. Two more fell, the other lead warrior and one man in the column.

It worked perfectly. Instantly the Indians broke for shelter, charging the hill behind which lay Davis and the company.

They came on a dead run, and Davis let them come. At point-blank range he fired. A crashing volley hit the charging Indians and those in the lead went down in a wild melee of screaming, wounded horses and yelling Indians. Firing coolly, Company C poured lead into the mass below. And then the Indians were out and running.

Scattered shots, then silence. Corporal Patton came up at a dead run and swung down. He saluted swiftly. "Silvers gone, sir. Tangled with a 'Pache and both of 'em gone, sir."

"Thanks, Corporal. Get set. They'll be back."

There was sporadic firing, and Davis studied the meadow and the slope. The ambush had taken seventeen Indians and half again that many horses. A number of wounded had been carried away.

He studied the grassy plain where the Indians had disappeared. There was a faint stirring of the grass. He fired into the grass and saw an Indian half rise, then sink back.

He studied the situation. Nothing more to be gained here by sniping fire. In any event, they had taught Vittoro a lesson.

"Sergeant?"

"Yes, sir?"

"Get the horses. We'll move on."

Clanahan's voice boomed. "Lieutenant! *Look!*"

Davis wheeled and saw the rider. At first he thought it was an Apache, and then he knew no Indian ever rode like that. The man was hunkered down low and riding hard, but he had stirrups and there was a flash of sunlight on polished leather, and then he recognized the horse.

The rider was coming at a dead run and he did not slow up until he had plunged into the very circle of soldiers. Then he drew up sharply, his horse rearing high, and he slid to the ground. It was Pete Britton.

His hard old face was gray and there was blood on his shirt. "Lieutenant," his voice was calm, "you got more'n a hundred Mimbreños comin' up behind you."

Lieutenant Creyton C. Davis stood very still. He had his hat in his hand and he felt the wind stirring his hair. "What chance of getting through to the fort, Pete?"

"Not none a-tall." Pete Britton hesitated, then he said quietly, "I caught me a brave. He wasn't so brave an' he talked. He said forty Mescaleros left the reservation last night. There's more Mimbreños comin', too. You're boxed in, Lieutenant. My guess is what we know ain't but part of it. I figure half the Apache nation is betwixt us an' the fort."

"Could you get through?"

"Might."

"I want a message taken."

Old Pete spat into the dust, then he grinned slowly. "Lieutenant, git yo'self another boy. I got a crease in my hide back yonder. I ain't fixed for ridin'. Anyway, I've took a lot of 'Pache hair in my time. I'll give 'em a chance at mine."

Davis put on his hat. "All right, Pete. Glad to have you."

"They'll know soon enough," Pete said dryly. "Anyways, I'm agittin' rheumatic these days. Figure I'd like it better thisaway."

Lieutenant Davis turned to Breen. "All right, Sergeant. Have the boys dig in and get settled. We'll wait for them."

Wind stirred the grass. Sweat trickled down his face. He shook his canteen. It was over half full. They moved back to the rim of the hills around the tiny basin where the horses were held.

There was dust to the south, and away there to the east there was dust. He mopped his brow and waited. He took the letter to his wife from his pocket and thrust it conspicuously over a spear of bear grass.

He settled down and lighted a smoke. Clanahan was squatted on his heels and he grinned at the Lieutenant. "Wished I had a drink," he said. "I could get drunk without makin' the guardhouse."

Davis turned and reached into his saddlebag. He drew out a flat bottle and tossed it to the burly Irishman.

Clanahan grinned and caught the bottle in his big palm. The pulled cork made a comfortable sound. He tilted back his head and drank.

There was no sound but the wind, no movement but the bending grass.

FIVE

H ondo Lane walked the lineback into the willows and let the horse plunge his dark muzzle into the cold, clear water of the stream.

Day had come but the sun was obscured behind towering masses of thunderheads. The morning was cool. There was no wind.

Two days out of Angie Lowe's ranch and he had just reached the bank of Little Dutch Creek. At this rate he would be four days getting to the post. If he got there at all.

Twice on the first day he had cut the trail sign of small Apache bands. Yesterday, after swinging wide to try to avoid further meetings, he had narrowly escaped being seen on a grassy hillside.

Luckily he had left the lineback in an arroyo over the ridge, so he flattened out in the grass and lay unmoving, and so unseen.

Thunder rumbled like the booming of far-off guns. The cumulus had darkened. Hondo flattened beside the stream, drank, then filled his canteen. Sam had crossed the stream and was drinking there. His head came up sharply, muzzle dripping water.

Hondo caught the lineback's nostrils and held them.

Two Mescaleros came up the creek, one of them riding a big chestnut horse with a U.S. brand. The other wore a lieutenant's blue coat, now dusty and darkly stained.

Not twelve feet away they stopped. Hondo slid his bowie knife into his hand. A gun would be more certain, but how far away were other Indians? He took a quick, sure step.

The Mescaleros turned like cats and he lunged. The nearest Indian struck down barehanded at the knife blade . . . too late. The blade went in hard and Lane jerked it across and free. The Mescalero grabbed his wrist and pulled Hondo down, dying under him.

Jerking free, Hondo rolled over, and then he saw that the other Indian was down. Over him, humped in awful fury, was Sam. The big dog had sprung from close up, and the startled Apache had no chance with ninety pounds of snarling, driving fury on top of him.

Lane scrambled to his feet and put a hand on the dog. "All right, Sam."

Reluctantly the dog let go. There was a long scratch on his ribs. Ears pricked, still growling, he walked stiff-legged around the dying Indian, then at another word from Hondo he turned and went into the cold water, lying down.

Lane peeled bridle and blanket from the horse with the Army brand and turned it loose. There was a bloody scratch on the flank not yet a day old.

The Mescalero with the officer's coat had something else. Hondo stooped and pulled it from the pocket. The guidon of Company C, trampled, dusty, and bloody.

He stepped into the leather and moved off, riding with caution. There was a faint stirring in the grass now, and there was a smell of dampness in the air. Sam moved far out on the flank, trotting with his head up, knowing the danger.

Then he saw the buzzards. They were low down over a distant hill. He put the lineback into a trot, and then, turning in the saddle, he looked back. Only the long grass moved, only the distant hills lined the horizon.

He inhaled deeply, liking the cool, fresh air. He rode down into the long valley down which the Apaches had come.

At least eighty warriors, likely more. Davis had been outnumbered two to one. He puckered his brow. The Indians had been moving right along, not like men going into battle.

The first thing he saw was a dead pony. He drew up, scanning the ground. He counted nine more, moved ahead, and saw too many to count. There was blood on the grass where men had fallen. He saw a spot of white. It was a dead trooper, stripped and mutilated.

Swinging right into the hills, he saw several brass cartridge cases. Two, three men here. He saw it then. Ambush. Not by the Indians, but by Lieutenant Davis and Company C. And they had hit hard at the moving Apaches.

On the opposite hill, toward which the Apaches had fled for shelter, he saw more horses and several spots of white.

Atop the hill he drew up, looking around. He saw all that remained of Company C, the naked bodies of the dead, fallen in their blood and their glory as fighting men should. Some were scalped, many were not.

Lieutenant Davis had been shot three times, twice through the body, then a finishing shot through the head. His body was not mutilated. Neither was that of big Clanahan, lying close by.

They had died together, the lieutenant and the malcontent.

Nearby lay a broken whisky bottle. Hondo Lane rolled a smoke and lit it, knowing what had happened here. That bottle had belonged to Davis, and at the end he must have given it to Clanahan. Hondo could picture the scene . . . the Lieutenant giving the bottle to the man he had several times sent to the guardhouse for drunken brawling, but a man who died well beside an officer he understood.

He drew deep on the cigarette. This was no place to stop. Yet he hesitated, looking for the one man who should be here. He saw him then, some thirty yards away.

Old Pete Britton had outlasted them all. That was evident from the scattered shells around his body. Despite the Apache's need for weapons, the two rifles he had used were not taken.

His body was unmutilated. These were signs of respect paid by the Apaches to a fighting man.

Judging by the signs, the old man must have held out at least an hour longer than the others. On his hard old face there was a taunting, wolfish grin. He had defeated his ancient fears of loneliness, sickness, and poverty.

Only when he was once more in the saddle did he see the fleck of white on the blade of bear grass. It was a thick letter, addressed to Mrs. Martha Davis.

Turning down the valley, he saw the rest of the story. The ambush had worked, a decisive blow if not a conclusive victory. And then the Mimbreños had come up from behind. The unknown factor. . . .

Briefly he scouted around, reading the last grim details of the story, written plainly here. Then he started the lineback down the long valley at a steady trot. So it had started, then, and with a crashing victory for the Apaches. Yet a victory that had cost them much. The Apaches carried off their dead and wounded, but there were bloodstains on the grass and many of them marked where men had died.

He rubbed the scrabble of beard on his jaws, staring bleakly into the west. He felt the stir of wind upon his neck, the grass bent around him, and the lineback's mane streamed away, and with the wind came a few large, scattered drops of rain.

Turning, the slap of rain against his hard cheeks, he dug into the bedroll for his slicker. When he had it on, he kept to low ground, off the hills where lightning would strike. And then came the rain and the wind. It struck with a solid blow. There was an instant of pause, then the downpour. Thunder roared in the distance, then lightning snapped at the ridge to his right and there was a smell of brimstone and charred grass.

The lineback moved out, wanting to run, and he let it go. The rain roared down and the wind swept it along the grass. In a matter of minutes there was a trickle of brown water down the valley, then a widening rush. He moved the horse to ground a few feet higher and pushed on.

Suddenly an arroyo cut the ground across before him. Already the sand was damp and there was a trickle of water. He hesitated, hearing the roar of the water coming downstream, knowing that wall of rolling water would be upon him in seconds. Then he gambled.

He put the lineback down the bank and slapped him hard on the hip. The startled animal leaped from under him, and, snorting in terror, was running, belly down, across the arroyo. Almost in the middle he saw the wall of water upstream, bearing great logs on its crest. Bank to bank the rolling wall of brown water rushed at him, and he slapped spurs to the lineback and the horse gave a pain-maddened lunge and reached the bank. Its hoofs slipped in the clay, then caught, and with two great bounds the horse was up and away from the water.

"Good boy." Hondo patted the horse's shoulder. "You'll do to take along."

The horse tossed his head impatiently and they pushed on. Rain pelted them, the sod turned soggy underfoot, waves of wind washed over them, and great whips of lightning lashed the darkened hills. Stones glistened like gems, and the gray veil of the rain strained out the distance and left nothing but the wet and roaring world through which they moved, man and horse, joined now before the common terror of the storm.

A dozen times he turned aside, working away from torrents of white water roaring down arroyos. Once he saw a great cottonwood uprooted and lying upon its side. He saw tall grass flattened to the ground, and hail beat upon them, then passed.

There was no stopping, for there was no place to stop. He rode on, half stunned by the driving fury of the storm, remembering the house in the basin and wondering how Angie fared. She should have a man. It was not good for a woman to live alone. Nor a man.

And that boy . . . The lad needed a father.

From a low place in the hills his eye caught a glistening something, and he reined over and rode nearer. It was a low roof, a stone-faced dugout in the side of a hill. He rode the horse down and, swinging down, opened the door. It was roomy and dry within.

It was a struggle to get the horse through the door, but he made it. At the back of the dugout there was a dirt-floored cave where there was a hitch rail and a trough. He shucked out of his slicker and took wood from a pile of mesquite roots and built a fire in the crude fireplace. There was a little grain left in the bag brought from Angie's, and he hung a feed bag on the horse, then wiped him as dry as possible.

The fire blazed up, the room grew warm. Hondo barred the door and fixed a meal, then lay down on the boards of the bunk and dozed. The firelight played on his face, the rain roared and pounded on the roof overhead.

What kind of man could leave a woman like that in Apache country? His eyes were suddenly wide open and he was angry, thinking about it. She was all woman, that one. And a person . . . a real person.

Somewhere along the tangled trail of his thoughts he dropped off and slept, and while he slept the rain roared on, tracks were washed out, and the bodies of the silent men of Company C lay wide-eyed to the rain and bare-chested to the wind, but the blood and the dust washed away, and the stark features of Lieutenant Davis stared at the sky, where the lightning played and the fury of the storm worried its way out. Lieutenant Creyton C. Davis, graduate of West Point, veteran of the Civil War and the Indian wars, darling of Richmond dance floors, hero of a Washington romance, dead now in the long grass on a lonely hill, west of everything.

The fire smoldered and blinked its light away, finding no fuel, and in the cold sundown Hondo Lane opened his eyes and looked up at the roof, and then swung his feet down.

The rain was gone. There was no wind. Out there all was silent. He opened the door and stepped out. Broken clouds floated above, and in the far-off west the storm rolled and grumbled like a drunken sergeant in his sleep.

Lane led out his horse and tightened the cinch, then stepped into the saddle again and followed westward, after the storm.

And the storm clouds were topped with fire, spears of crimson shot out, piercing the tall sky, and a star appeared. It was cool now, and still.

The miles fell behind. In the distance there was faint smoke, then came the rain-washed walls of the village and the rain-darkened parade ground, the sutler's store and the home of the Army west of the Rio Grande.

Hondo Lane pulled his hat brim lower and started the lineback down the slope. At least, he thought, this is still here.

But behind this thought there was the memory of a quiet-faced woman and a child, of a house beside a stream, and of a woman moving in the house while he slept. He shifted rest-lessly in the saddle and swore at the horse to cover his feeling and his wonder at it.

SIX

The storm, sweeping westward across the vast reach of desert and mountain, had crossed the little ranch in the basin before it reached Hondo Lane and the bodies of Company C's fallen veterans. It had come roaring out of the sky, driving before it a barrage of rain that pelted the dry soil, lifting dust as it struck, and bringing to the air that peculiar odor that comes when rain first strikes dry ground.

Not even the cliff protected the cabin from the force of the storm, or from the roar of thunder but it was filled with warmth, comfort, and the smell of coffee. But it was a house empty, for the man was gone.

The sound of rushing water in the usually dry wash frightened her a little, for she had seen those torrents move all before them, and had seen them come when the sky was clear above, and rain only over the distant mountains. Yet now the rain was general, and the parched earth of her garden drank it eagerly.

Some water would remain in the hollow behind the washed-out dam, too. It would last a few weeks, enough so she could irrigate several times, and so it might be the difference between a good crop and none at all.

59

Johnny was unnaturally quiet, watching her, his face serious. "Will the man come back, Mommy?"

"I don't know Johnny. He's very busy."

The same question was haunting her own thoughts. Would he return? And why should he? But if he did, what would she do?

The thought disturbed her. Why should she think of doing anything? What was there to do?

Worried by her own feelings, she sorted clothes for washing, then dusted and mopped, doing work she had not planned to do, merely to keep her thoughts occupied. Yet she kept wondering about him. Had he found shelter?

Remembering the incidents of his visit, she tried to tell herself that he was hard, cruel. His attitude toward the dog, toward Johnny . . . all of it. Yet in her heart she knew he was not cruel. Hard, yes. But how else could he be? And how deep did the hardness go?

What lessons he had learned had come to him in a bitter school. It was the way he knew of learning, a hard way but a fast way that taught its lessons well. She remembered the way he had come off the pallet, gun in hand. What life had a man lived who could be so alert, even in sleep?

It was nearly sundown when the rain ended at the basin, and she went outside. The air was miraculously cool and washed clean and clear. To breathe it was like drinking cold water. The sky was still a broken mass of cloud, and thunder rumbled off in the canyon of the faraway western hills. Lowering masses of cloud filled the hollows of the hills and nestled in the saddles where the ridge dipped low. Occasionally the bulging domes of cloud flared incandescent with distant lightning.

Leaves dripped, water whispered against the banks of the wash, brown and swirling. She fed the horses and stood silent in the yard, looking around at the hills. He was gone. Even his tracks were gone. What kind of woman was she, a married woman and a mother, to be thinking like this of any man?

A man who had gone as if he had never been. But that was not true. His footprints were gone from the yard, yet some-

thing remained, something intangible, yet present. A something that set her heart yearning toward the way his horse had
gone, that made her remember the way he walked, the strange,
somber, almost lonely expression of his eyes. The hunger in
them when she had looked up suddenly and met his gaze . . .
She flushed, remembering it. And the way he had kissed her,
and what he had said.

"A woman walks with her head up ought to kiss a man
before she dies."

She repeated the words, feeling the heavy beat of her heart.
What a strange thing to say to a woman! And the way he had
kissed her . . . not fierce, not possessive, not demanding, and
yet so much much more.

Slow drops from the eaves fell into the barrel placed to catch
the runoff. In the late dusk the hills were unnaturally green
and lovely after the rain. She would take the horses out to the
hills in the morning and picket them on the grass where she
could keep watch on them from the garden. She walked to the
corral and put her hand on the wet top rail and looked again at
the hills. The hills etched themselves against the sky darkening
and gray. It would be lonely now, lonely as never before.

She turned quickly from the thought gathering her skirt in a
quick gesture and biting her lip against sudden tears. She
brushed them away hastily and, squaring her shoulders, walked
to the house. Yet in the door, as if reluctant to close it finally
against the night where he had gone, she turned again to look
toward the hills. And the silent hills lay still. Even in the
moments of her walking their green had gone, and the dark
wings of night shadowed the basin.

She closed the door and dropped the bar in place. It was no
use to think. He was a man with his life to live, a man who had
stopped for a night, bought a horse, and ridden away. Other
men had come and gone. He was no different . . . yet he was.

This was her home. She had no time for pilgrim thoughts to
go wandering away over the hills after a strange rider. She had
a home and a son. It was like her that she no longer thought of
Ed. She did not believe him killed, but he would not come

back, not unless he were hurt and running. He was out of her life . . . a boy who had taken vows it took a man to keep.

And a woman.

And keep them she had. Only now he was gone, and their marriage was a shadow thing that had left only Johnny behind it. And even here Ed seemed to have failed; he was a man who left his mark upon nothing, not even upon his son.

It was enough to think of her son, enough to see that he grew tall and strong, that he became a citizen of his land, a father of children in his time, that he learned to build instead of destroy, that he learned to use the land and protect it, not waste the wealth it gave. This was her mission, her problem.

There was something her father had said. "We do not own the land, Angie. We hold it in trust for tomorrow. We take our living from it, but we must leave it rich for your son and for his sons and for all of those who shall follow."

Yet as she put supper on the table her thoughts were not upon the land. They were hearing the creak of a saddle and a big man's slow voice, quiet in the room.

And when she lay in bed and drew the blankets high, she looked up into the darkness and remembered Johnny's question. "Will the man come back, Mommy?"

The morning was nearly gone when Angie took the two buckets and walked to the well. The sun was high, and only a few lost tufts of cottony cloud floated in the wide sky. All morning she had worked steadily around the house, only going out to feed the horses and to check the amount of water behind the dam. There was not so much as she had hoped, but enough to irrigate her garden several times. She had cleared mud away from the gate her father had built so the water would be free to flow when it was opened. Her decision to take the horses to the hills had been changed in favor of discretion. She did not believe the Apaches would ever bother her, but horses were a temptation she did not intend to make too inviting.

She filled the first bucket, then the second. She heard no

sound, and was standing looking toward the hills when something made her turn.

An Indian had come from the trees and sat the back of his rough-looking paint pony, staring at her. She had heard no sound, no movement.

Another appeared, and then another. And then they began to materialize from the trees as though by magic until there were a dozen.

She had seen them ride by, from time to time she had seen them at the spring, yet this was the first time she had seen so many at such close range.

They were men of medium height who seemed shorter than their height because of wide shoulders and deep chests. Most of their faces were flat-lipped and cruel, but all were sinewy and powerful in build, dark-skinned and dusty now, their lank black hair hanging to their shoulders, bound only with headbands.

One of these men sat a very striking pony, and by his looks, Angie knew him for their leader. Her eyes looked past him at a tall, evil-looking Apache who whispered something to the older man, who seemed to be a chief. From the mane of the tall Indian hung several strips of bloody flesh and hair. Scalps, and none of them more than a day old.

She felt herself turn faint and sick, but she forced herself to stand straight. Pale and frightened, she nevertheless managed to keep her voice strong as she spoke to the older man.

"You are Vittoro."

"I am the one who is called Vittoro."

"Your horses have watered here."

His flat black eyes made no change. His face might have been hewn from mahogany.

"You were warned."

"I could not leave. My husband is away. And this is my home."

Vittoro looked at her, and the Indians waited. A vagrant breeze caught at the drying dust of the yard and it swirled briefly, then died. The cottonwoods rustled among themselves.

"This is an Apache spring."

"The Apaches live in the mountains," Angie replied. "They do not need this spring. I have a son. I do need it."

"But when the Apache comes this way, where shall he drink? His throat is dry. You would keep him from water."

"There is water yonder." She pointed to the hills. "But if the people of Vittoro come in peace, they may drink. When have I denied them?"

Vittoro's voice was shaded with impatience, and with a stab of fear she knew that talking was over.

"It is sworn there will be no whites in Apache territory." He turned on the tall Indian. "Silva!" He spoke rapidly in the Apache tongue, and Angie saw the quick grin on Silva's face. The tall Indian slid from his pony. He touched the mane of Vittoro's palomino and said something, evidently comparing it with the color of Angie's hair. Then he drew his knife and started toward her.

She did not scream. She could not. Nor would she let them see her fear. She stood straighter, putting contempt in her face. And then Johnny came out of the door.

He had the Walker Colt. He was holding the big pistol up and pointing it at Silva.

Silva stopped, and one of the Indians chuckled. Even Silva grinned at the ludicrous sight of the boy holding a pistol nearly as large as himself, and so obviously determined.

Angie wheeled and started for the rifle on the porch, but an Indian grabbed her from behind. As he did so, the gun bellowed.

The gun was tipped high, and when it went off the bullet creased Silva's scalp, knocking him down. Johnny, knocked backward by the kick of the huge pistol, also fell.

Jerking loose from the Indian who held her, Angie ran to Johnny. Silva lay still on the ground, unconscious.

Vittoro sat his pony his face showing no expression. He looked at the boy. "You are the mother of a strong son," he said quietly. "It is well you have no man. You might raise an army of warriors to fight my people."

"I have no wish to fight your people." Angie spoke with

dignity. "Your people have your ways, I have mine. I live in peace when I am left in peace. I did not think," her chin lifted, "that the great Vittoro made war upon women!"

Vittoro slid from his horse and drew his knife. Angie clutched her son, wishing she had picked up the pistol, knowing now it would do no good. There was nothing anyone could do now.

He walked toward them, a bigger man than she had believed, and every inch the chief. The Indians behind him sat their horses in silence.

Vittoro picked up Johnny's hand and knicked his thumb with the point of the knife, then his own. He pressed them together, their blood mingling.

"He is my blood brother. I name him Small Warrior, of the Moon Dog Lodge of the Chiricahua Apache." He looked at Angie, a flicker of something that might have been kindness in his eyes. "You will care for him well. As mother of a Chiricahua warrior, you may live here in safety."

Silva came swiftly to his feet, staring around. He put a hand to his head. It came away bloody. Knife in hand, he started forward, but Vittoro spoke sharply. Sulking, Silva turned and strode to his pony.

Angie clutched Johnny. Vittoro swung to the back of the palomino. "I knew you were a great warrior," she said. "I hope someday someone befriends your sons."

The iron face turned bleakly savage. "My sons are dead—in a white man's prison."

They rode swiftly off. Only Silva looked back, and Angie caught that look. From that day on she knew only Vittoro stood between her and the shame and anger of Silva. And she knew the story of Silva's defeat would be told in the villages, and his hate would harden to an evil thing.

She lifted the pistol from the ground. It had been loaded. Even when he was not with them, Hondo Lane had been the reason of their security. It was he that had advised her, and had loaded the pistol.

SEVEN

B eyond the sprawling villages of adobes and jacales were the neatly ranged tents of the cavalry unit, and beside them and forming two sides of the square were the sutler's store, the quartermaster's storehouse, the bakery, the headquarters building, the blacksmith shop, and the stables. None of these were imposing structures. All looked squalid and dismal even after the bathing of rain.

A few scouts and frontier drifters lounged in the area near the sutler's store, or sat on the steps before it. They watched the lone rider come down the slope and ventured guesses as to who he was and where he came from. It was not a time to be riding alone, and not many were willing to chance it. Not even the hardy souls who loitered around the sutler's store.

A man came to the door of a jacal, a structure of upright logs set in holes in the ground and plastered with mud, roofed with smaller branches and more mud. He stared at the rider. He said something over his shoulder and another face appeared in the door of the jacal, and then both men walked out.

It took little to get men out of the jacales, places more suited to the residence of scattered and indifferent centipedes, scorpions, or occasional tarantulas than of human beings.

"Him, all right." Dick spat tobacco juice at an unoffending lizard and chuckled. "Knowed it."

Hondo walked the lineback to the hitch rail and swung down. Sam stopped a few feet away looking at the scouts without pleasure. He did not even pant. He just sat and stared glumly.

"Well," said Buffalo, a huge, whiskered man in a greasy buckskin shirt. "I owe you a jug of redeye. Settle come payday." He walked around the dog. "That dog's as friendly as a puma."

He looked carefully at the lineback, noting the strangeness of the horse. His eyes were sharp and attentive and as quick to see and catalogue as the eyes of an Apache. Hondo Lane had been places and none of it had been easy. It showed where the scout could see it.

"Figured your hair would be hanging in some Apache wicki-up. Bet Dick on it. You're sure a disappointment to me, Hondo."

"You like to won. I wore out some horses."

"You wore out you, while you was at it," Dick said. "Lemme get that war bag."

Headquarters building was a structure of adobe and rough planks identified by the flagpole. A sergeant sat behind a box that did duty for a desk. An enlisted cavalryman and a scout sat on a bench against the wall.

A tall, rather handsome young man with a petulant, irritable expression was addressing the sergeant. He was a lean-bodied man with a low-tied gun and something of the dress of a frontier dandy, limited only by his cash outlay.

"I say I got a right to talk to this here bowneck major." His voice was casually insolent. "I don't talk to no underlings."

"The Major's sleeping." The sergeant spoke in a careful, noncommittal tone. His manner betrayed all too clearly that he spoke to a civilian, to a man he disliked, and to a man he would cheerfully throw out of the office if it were permitted. At the same time, he spoke with the exasperated patience of a man who knows he must keep peace with citizens.

"That's too bad about him. I'm a citizen and I want to see him."

"Major Sherry ain't slept for three days. I can tell you everything just as well as him. We ain't heard nothin' from up north."

The lean-hipped rider stared at him with contempt. "If you ask me, the Cavalry's scared of Vittoro. And I think the U.S. Cavalry . . ."

Major Sherry came in from the room behind the sergeant. He was a tall man, wire-taut and strong, but his face was lined and exhausted. The speaker, suddenly aware of his presence, let his voice die away.

"I am greatly interested in your opinion of the United States Cavalry," Major Sherry said dryly. "Continue, Mr. Whatever-your-name-is."

"I'm Ed Lowe," the lean-hipped man said. His voice lost its irritation before the sharpness of the Major's and became complaining. "The Cavalry's supposed to support the settlers. I've got some cattle up north and I—"

"Company C is making a sweep to the north to escort out any settlers they may find. Company C is over a week late in returning. That is all I am able to tell you."

Hondo came through the door behind Lowe, followed by Sam. The big dog sank to the floor just inside the door. Hondo crossed and hung his saddle on the wall beside several other saddles. When the saddle was hung he looked back over his shoulder.

"C Company won't be back."

He turned slowly, as if reluctant to give them the news, and on the desktop before the sergeant he dropped the crumpled, bloodstained guidon of C Company.

Major Sherry stared at the guidon, his face growing stiff and old. Crey Davis. . . . He would have to tell his wife. Why the hell did he ever volunteer for the Arizona command?

The story was there. Hondo would provide the details, but actually, none were needed except for the reports. Suddenly, wearily, Major Sherry knew he would rather not hear them. Good friends gone . . . good soldiers, good fighting men. C Company had been his best, his toughest outfit.

Looking up, he saw Ed Lowe. A flicker of disgust showed, and he said irritably, "You may leave. I have business to attend to."

Major Sherry's head came around. "Sergeant!"

The implication was plain and the sergeant came to his feet abruptly. He started around the desk. "Git!" he said. "An' don't come botherin' around no more!"

Lowe turned angrily and started to the door. Hondo had moved back to the wall to hang up his pistol belt. Lowe found himself facing the big dog, and although there was plenty of room to pass, his anger flamed suddenly. "Get out of the way, you mangy cur!" He drew his foot back.

Sam came to his feet with a swift, almost catlike move, crouched, his muscles bunched to leap. His lips curled back from his teeth but he neither growled nor snarled, only looked up at Lowe, his face ugly with readiness.

Taken aback by the sudden reaction, Ed Lowe stepped back. Then he reached for his gun.

Hondo's gun belt was on the hook but his Winchester was in his hand. He tipped the barrel forward with his left hand slapping the butt into his hand. The butt struck his hand and at almost the same instant his thumb cocked the hammer back. Lowe froze at the sharp click, turning his head.

There was no mistaking the rifle. It was hip-high and the muzzle was aimed at his stomach and not eight feet away. Ed Lowe looked at the rifle and his eyes lifted to the bleak, wind-raw face of Hondo Lane. Something in Ed Lowe seemed to back up and sit down.

"If that's your cur, get him out of the way."

Hondo neither advised nor threatened. "Walk around him."

"I'll be hanged if I ever go out of my way for a cur dog!"

Lane's face did not change. His voice was matter of fact. "Man should always do what he thinks he should."

A fly buzzed in the room. Outside somewhere a horse stamped and there was a clang of iron on iron. Ed Lowe stood very still.

He did not know this man. He might be anybody. Yet there was something in his manner that was too calm, too casual. Ed Lowe was a good man with a gun and had found occasions to demonstrate it. He figured there were few better. Yet suddenly he was examining his hole card and he did not like what he saw.

There was that in the attitude of the stranger that implied all too much familiarity with such situations. Ed Lowe's thoughts probed his memory for the face, for something that would be a clue. He liked to know what he was going up against.

Nor did he like the obvious satisfaction in the sergeant's face. The sergeant would not be unhappy to see him dead, and the sergeant seemed all too sure that he was about to see just that. And Ed Lowe did not have the kind of guts it would take to find out.

The blue fly buzzed. Somebody laughed in the outer air, and the flickering instant of hesitation was ended. Ed Lowe had been fairly called and he knew it. All he had to do was to gamble. . . . Suddenly sick and empty inside, Ed Lowe stepped around the dog and went blindly through the door.

For an instant there was silence and the sergeant sighed briefly, with genuine regret. "Thought maybe we'd be rid of him," he said to nobody in particular. "He's got it coming."

Hondo pushed the dog aside with his foot. "Don't block the door," he said quietly.

Major Sherry gestured to the guidon. "Where did you get this?"

"About half a day's ride south of Twin Buttes."

"How?"

"Off two Indians. Running Dog Lodge of the Mescaleros."

"So the Mescaleros are up, too. That makes all the Apache lodges."

Hondo shoved his hat back and began to build a smoke.

"Went up there," he said, "and backtrailed them Mescaleros.

Davis ambushed Vittoro. Figure he got twenty or more. He was pullin' out of the ambush when they hit him from behind. 'Nother outfit, maybe a hundred strong. He never had a chance."

"All there?"

"Yes. They got no prisoners, if that's what you mean." Hondo hesitated, and then said quietly, "Clanahan fought 'em off Davis' body at the end. They went out together, him an' the Lieutenant."

"Clanahan?" The Major's eyes brightened a little. He remembered the man, a big, black-haired Irishman with a brutal face. A drunk, a brawler, a troublemaker, but a fighter. And he was Army. "He was a good man."

Hondo described the action briefly as he had seen the sign on the ground. It was a clear, accurate picture and had its value. Every battle was a lesson; in each there was something to be learned. Major Sherry never ceased to marvel at what these men would read from the ground, yet he had seen their facts proved too many times to doubt them.

"They won," Hondo said, "but it hurt. They got hit hard."

He took a long drag on his cigarette and turned to the door, then paused. "Any settlers out of the north basin since I been away? Lately?"

"A few."

"Handsome woman? Fair? With a small boy, maybe six years old?"

"No. All middle-aged or elderly people."

Hondo Lane walked to the door and found Buffalo waiting with his war bag. He reached for it but Buffalo pushed his hand away. "I'll tote it."

Hondo walked out into the cool of the evening. They had not come out, then. He had hoped that after he had gone Angie would change her mind. She could have made it through while he rode north to follow through on the story of Company C. But there was nothing.

Buffalo walked along beside Hondo, shifting the war bag to his other hand. "Old Pete Britton was scoutin' with C Company. Wintered with Pete oncet up on the Divide. Ornery cuss."

"Last of them," Hondo said. "Maybe an hour, alone on a hilltop."

They walked on in silence. At the door of the jacal where Hondo stopped, Buffalo put down the bag.

"Old Pete, he worried himself a lot. That winter on the Divide he was laid up lot of the time. Rheumatic, he was. Skeered of being crippled."

They stood together and smoked quietly. Hondo explained about the body. Buffalo dropped his cigarette, then walked away, saying no more. Hondo stood alone then, looking into the night.

He was no man to be thinking about a woman. He had never lived with a woman . . . wouldn't know how to. He wouldn't know how to handle a kid, either. And women . . . It was one thing with a squaw. After a while you knew them. But a girl like Angie, now, that would be different. He was a fool to even think about it. What did he have to offer a woman?

He sat down in the doorway and took off his boots. He saw a soldier coming down the line of tents. It was the same trooper that had been in the headquarters building.

"That fellow, complaining to the Major. Who was he?"

The trooper hesitated, liking the big man and ready to talk. "Don't know his name."

"Why doesn't he go in?"

"Same reason he walked around your dog when you told him." He waited, wanting to talk, hesitating. "Them Indians you took that C pennant off'n. Dead Indians?"

"Finally."

He got up and turned inside. The trooper stood outside in the dark, a faint shadow in the greater darkness of the night.

The cot creaked. Almost at once there were snores. The soldier stood alone, looking into the night, thinking of a night in his own little New England village. A night like this, cool, quiet. . . .

There had been a girl there. He could not even remember

her name, just a quiet, pretty girl. He wished he could remember. He would like to write her a letter.

He thought of Company C, lying under the rain, and under
the stars.

A man needed somebody to think about, he needed somebody somewhere. . . .

EIGHT

I t was after ten when Hondo awakened. Accustomed to sleeping in short snatches, when and where it was possible, his
body could not attune itself to long, unrestricted rest. To
oversleep was dangerous, and despite his weariness, he awakened
suddenly and with a start.

He stared up into the dark, not moving until his mind knew
where he was and the countless tiny sounds began to sort and
adjust themselves. Slowly his muscles relaxed. He was at the
post.

Groggily he sat up and ran his fingers through his hair. His
body felt heavy and his mouth tasted bad. He swore, walked to
the bucket on the table, and lifted it to drink, then he spat into
the street.

It was very dark but there were stars. A coolness left by the
rain still pervaded the desert night. He bathed his face, combed
his hair, and then picked up his hat. From up the company
street he heard the sound of an out-of-tune piano, and with it a
clear Irish tenor singing "Brennan on the Moor," an old Irish
folk song of a highwayman and his love.

Hondo Lane stepped out into the night and looked around,
sensing the darkness, taking his feel of it before moving on. Far

out over the hills a coyote yapped his loneliness to the listening stars. A faint breeze stirred the tent flaps. A tent not far away showed the dull glow of a lamp and he heard a murmur of voices and a slap of cards.

Hondo Lane walked up the street toward the sutler's store, his boots grating on the gravel and clay of the parade ground. Two men sat outside the store, smoking. One of them murmured a greeting, and Hondo replied with a short "Howdy," not knowing the man.

Inside the room was crowded. It was a long and dingy room without color, without light, without women. Several men leaned against the homemade bar at one end. At the other there was a counter where trade goods were dispensed, with shelves behind it.

The Irish tenor leaned on the battered upright piano, wearing a rumpled but once fashionable gray suit and a derby hat with a dent and a badly scuffed brim. He was a young man with a dashing mustache, and he needed a shave. The man at the piano was a cow hand, bearing out the fact that in the melting pot of the West there was no estimating the hidden talents of a drifting man.

All were roughly dressed but the soldiers. A few were still around, although most had turned in by now. The men of the crowd were cow hands, cattlemen, gamblers, prospectors, drifters, and scouts. There was a tension in the group, and nobody was talking of what they were all thinking. In the morning a burial party would go out to inter the bodies of Company C—a party that must in itself be strong. Not a man here but might be called upon to go, and not a man here who had not lost a friend or drinking companion in the massacre of Company C.

Hondo walked to the bar and the sutler reached underneath for a bottle of Irish whisky. He winked at Hondo, filled his glass, and said quietly, "On the house." Then the bottle vanished again, unseen by the habitués of the saloon and store.

Hondo looked around slowly. A card game was going at the other end of the room. Buffalo was sitting in, and Hondo recognized the man with whom he had had trouble at headquarters. There was another character of whom he had seen a good deal, not only here but at the Pass, over in Texas. A sour-faced man with a snaky look to his eyes and a habit of winning in poker games, no matter how. The last of them was Pete Summervel.

Pete was seventeen, a hard-riding youngster, cocky, over-confident. Now he was not quite drunk, but nearing it. Obviously he was in no condition to play poker, and obviously the gambler was encouraging him to drink. Hondo tossed off his own drink and watched the game. The man with whom he had had trouble earlier seemed adept with the cards. Hondo put down his glass, drew the back of his hand across his mouth, and walked over to the table.

Ed Lowe looked up when Hondo stopped by the table, and something in him tightened. "Three sixes and two pretty fours," he said, spreading his cards. "I win. Let's go again."

Pete looked up and grinned. "Hi, Hondo! Broke my heart when I heard you made it."

"Your pa know when you started going against that so-called whisky, Pete?"

Pete grinned. The whisky was already having its effect. "Ain't seen him for a month."

Hondo dropped his hand to his shoulder. "I know you haven't, an' I've got a message from him for you. Come on."

Pete got to his feet, staggering a little. "Sure Hondo."

"Come down to the bar where we can talk. These gents'll excuse you."

"I won't."

The words were low-spoken, but Hondo heard them clearly. He turned. It was the man with whom he had had trouble earlier.

"I'm out almost a hundred simoleans."

"That I can figure," Hondo replied mildly, "with Buffalo in the game. Come along, Pete."

Lowe came to his feet quickly and caught Hondo by the shirt front. "*Wait* a minute!"

Hondo looked at the hand gripping his shirt, then lifted his cold eyes to Lowe's. "I just bought that shirt," he said mildly. The other men were on their feet, too.

Hondo pushed Pete out of range as Lowe started a punch. It was the wrong thing for Lowe to do. As the punch started, Hondo's left hand came up and knocked the grip loose from his shirt and he stepped inside of the looping left with a lifting right uppercut to the chin.

Lowe staggered, and instantly Hondo swung a right that knocked Buffalo into a corner. Lowe had gone down hard, but as Buffalo sat up, Lowe gathered himself.

"What did you hit me for?" Buffalo demanded in pained surprise.

"Because you're the most dangerous."

Hondo had started to turn away when Lowe went for his gun. "Not in the back!" Buffalo shouted. "Leather it!"

Turning swiftly, Hondo kicked the gun from Lowe's hand, then he grabbed him by the shirt front and jerked him to his feet. Hondo smashed a right into Lowe's stomach, then shoved him away and hit him in the face with both hands. Lowe lunged, swinging, but Hondo knocked down Lowe's right and crossed over his left. Lowe staggered and Hondo walked in, his face expressionless. He hit Lowe with a left to the body, then a right.

Lowe backed up, not liking it, and Hondo slapped him. It was a powerful, brutal slap that jarred Lowe to his heels and turned him half around. Then Hondo dropped him with a straight right.

Lowe sprawled on the floor and Hondo picked him up by the scruff of the neck and the seat of the pants, and when somebody opened the door, he heaved him out into the dirt. Lowe landed on his face in the gravel and Hondo waited an instant in the door.

Ed Lowe rolled over. His body was alive with vindictive hatred and he stared up at Hondo. "You ain't heard the last of this!" he said thickly.

"Then I'll keep listenin'," Hondo said, turning back into the saloon. The door closed and Ed Lowe remained on the ground, staring at the blackness.

The two men seated outside had not moved. One's cigarette glowed red.

Lowe gathered himself and got shakily to his feet. He spat blood from a cut lip. His head felt foggy and there was a raw pain in his side. "I'll kill him!" he said into the night. "I'll kill him for this!"

The cigarette glowed briefly. "I was you," the voice said mildly, "I'd figure I was lucky he wasn't packin' a gun. That's Hondo Lane."

Inside, Hondo walked over to Buffalo. He put his hand on the big man's shoulder. "Sorry, friend. I didn't know who all was in that shindig an' I figured I wanted no part of you in a brawl."

Buffalo chuckled. "All right. I was wishin' the kid was out of it. Ed an' that sidewinder from the Pass roped him in."

Hondo jerked his head toward the door. "This is the second time I've tangled with that mouthy no-good. Who is he, anyhow?"

"Calls himself Lowe. Ed Lowe."

Ed Lowe. . . . Hondo looked at the glass on the bar. Angie's husband, and alive.

What kind of man would leave a woman and child alone at such a time as this? And he had been lifting the roof at headquarters about his cattle. Nothing said about his wife and child.

When F Company rode out of the post at daylight Hondo Lane was standing by to watch them go. With them was riding a company of scouts commanded by Lieutenant Crawford. These were a mixture of Apaches, Yaquis, Opatas, and Mexicans, with a scattering of Americans. All were skilled Indian fighters. It was a strong force for a burial detachment, but their orders were explicit. They were under no concern to attempt to follow Vittoro or to engage in any battle unless first attacked.

Hondo watched them go, his face somber. There was small chance they would encounter Vittoro, although the company of scouts carried enough wild-country brains to have found him no matter where he fled, if they had been permitted. The orders of Major Sherry had been definite, however, and he did not intend to overstep them unless the situation was drastic. To send good men after those who had died with Company C would be worse than foolish. When Crook was present in force, it would be a different story.

Hondo watched them ride out, then walked back to the jacal and began mending gear. He was thinking of Angie. It was no business of his. She had a husband. But she should not be out there alone.

Restlessly he went to the corral and curried the surprised lineback, then fed him a couple of carrots he found in a garden patch near the end of the village.

Buffalo wandered over and joined him. "Don't you be careless, Hondo," he advised. "That Lowe ain't liable to forget what you handed him last night."

"I won't forget."

He worked over the horse a little longer, then released him with a slap on the shoulder. As he watched the lineback cross the corral, he asked, "Lowe been around long?"

"Month, maybe more. Plays a little poker." Buffalo bit off a chew of tobacco. "Hangs out with that rattler Phalinger."

All day reports came in of moving Indians. Twenty Chiricahuas had left the reservation, all young bucks. Some Tontos had been seen crossing the Francisco River heading south. There was a gathering of the tribes.

Twice groups of settlers came into the post, worn and tired from travel, and found shelter in the abandoned tents of a departed Army unit. Each time Hondo made inquiries among them, but they had come in from farther south and there was no report of anyone in the Basin country. Restlessly he awaited return of the burial detail. They had no orders to go beyond the scene of the massacre, but the scouts would be riding over more country, and they might have some information.

It was unnaturally quiet at the post. There was no roistering or loud talk around the bar in the sutler's store. Men came and went hurriedly, and the mounted patrols that left the post moved in and out like clockwork. The last patrol in before dark reported a running battle with a handful of Indians in which one Indian was slain and a trooper wounded.

As the hours passed, tension grew. It was noon a day later before the burial detail rode in. No Indians had been seen, although they had cut the trails of several small groups.

Shortly after the burial detail returned, Hondo Lane walked into the headquarters building. The sergeant looked up as he entered.

"Major Sherry in?"

"He's in. Just a minute."

The sergeant returned. "Go on in. He said he wanted to see you, anyway."

Sherry was leaned back in his chair looking out the window at the heat-baked parade ground. He was a grim-faced, clean-cut man of forty-four, a professional soldier who knew the frontier and liked it. He knew the country, the Indians, and the men he commanded. Years of duty in face of the enemy had burned away all the spit and polish. He was a fighting man, and wanted to be nothing else. He had been close to the top of his class at the Point, but had never cared for Eastern duty. He knew the book on combat tactics, but most of what he knew had been learned by applying it in battle against enemies that could be counted the greatest guerrilla tacticians the world had ever known.

"What's on your mind, Lane?"

"I want to go out there." Lane jerked his head toward the hills. "Personal business."

Sherry turned to his desk and shuffled his papers. "Sorry, Lane. It can't be done. The General wants you here for the time being." He stacked the papers. "Personal business, you said?"

"Yes, sir. There's a woman out there, with a child. They wouldn't come in then. They might come now."

The Major took out his pipe and stoked it with tobacco. "You lived with the Apaches, that right?"

"Yes, sir."

Major Sherry touched a match to the pipe. "I've been ordered to hold all scouts in. The General has something in mind. Nevertheless, I'd like—and I know he'd like—some information on Vittoro. If anybody could get it, you could."

Hondo Lane shifted in his chair, waiting. The Major's face did not change.

"It's mighty dangerous out there. Any man who went out alone would be a fool. And we've orders to stop anyone—anyone at all."

Hondo Lane got to his feet and turned to the door. "That all, sir?"

"Yes." Major Sherry drew on his pipe and looked out the window. As Hondo pulled on his hat and opened the door, Sherry turned his face toward him. "Lane," he said quietly, "be careful."

NINE

A ngie came to the door to shake out her broom. She glanced
around the yard, but Johnny was not in sight. A thrill of
fright went through her, and she stepped out into the yard.
"Johnny! Johnny!"

There was no sound. Shading her eyes, she scanned the
hills. Johnny was an obedient child. He had been told not to go
to the hills, and so far he had always obeyed, going only when
they went together.

Frightened, she walked quickly around the house. He was
nowhere in sight.

"Johnny!"

Her call sounded, and the empty hills threw back her voice.
Her heart pounded heavily. She walked toward the corral.
"Johnny! Johnny!"

And then from the trees walked two horses. On one of them
was Vittoro, and Johnny rode the other.

Relief went over her like a cold shower, yet she looked
uncertainly at the hard-faced old Indian.

"Oh, I thought . . . I didn't know . . . I heard nothing."

"The Apache does not make noise."

The old Indian lifted Johnny to the ground, and his hands

82

were gentle, almost fatherly. A hand lingered on the boy's shoulder.

"Mommy, Vittoro says I'll make a good warrior."

The Apache nodded, starting the child toward his mother. "He will ride well and he does not fear."

"Look, Mommy. I have a headband."

Proudly he showed her the headband. There was an opal of exceptional beauty in the center.

She knelt to look at it. "How beautiful! And it has an opal!"

"It is the emblem of his lodge." Vittoro glanced at Johnny. "I speak with your mother. Go inside the house."

"Yes, Vittoro."

Obediently Johnny turned and ran into the house. Angie watched him, a little catch at her heart.

Vittoro looked at her and his eyes were serious. Mentally she stiffened, for instinctively she knew what was coming, and she knew that she must use every word with care. She had seen several parties of Indians pass, and she had seen the fresh scalps they carried. That she was alive only at the sufferance of Vittoro she knew. Whatever came, he must not be offended.

"A lodge should have a man. Small Warrior should have a father to instruct him."

"My husband will be home any day."

Vittoro considered this. Then he shook his head. "I do not think so. I think your man is dead. I will deliberate on this."

She hesitated, then said quietly, "It is the way of my people for a woman to choose her own man. If my man is dead, there will be another."

"Many braves ride with me."

"They follow a strong leader," she said, "but an Apache woman for an Apache man—a white woman for a white man."

Vittoro considered this. He said, "Small Warrior is blood brother to Vittoro. He must grow strong in the ways of Vittoro."

Her eyes looked frankly into those of the proud old man. "I would have it so. My son could have no better model than Vittoro. I had heard his greatness. Now I have known it—and he is also kind.

"My son," she continued slowly, "is born to this land. I would have him know it as the Apache knows it. The man I choose will teach him to know the ways of the Apache."

There was nothing to read in his face. He merely turned to his horse. "Of this I shall think," he said, and he walked his horse away into the trees.

For a long time after he was gone she stood perfectly still, forgetful of the hot sun, forgetful of the work that remained to be done.

An issue was before her, and she knew she walked a narrow way between life for herself and her son and death for them both. Yet she had not lied. She would like her son to know how to live off the country as the Apache did, yet he must remain true to his blood, true to his God, and true to his people and his country.

How long would Vittoro allow her to wait? Not long, that she knew. And then what remained for her? Unless the Army came, unless she escaped and abandoned her home, all she had in the world, then she must take a husband from among Vittoro's braves.

Yet what had she said? "The man I choose will teach him to know the ways of the Apache."

And who, of the men she knew, could do that? She blushed and bit her lip, unwilling to frame his name in her mind. Yet when she had taken up her broom again, she faced the fact of it. She had never been one to dodge issues. If she knew nothing else, she had learned in these lonely months to know herself, and she knew there was only one man of whom she could think in that way.

She was a woman still married, and she was thinking of Hondo Lane.

But what was it that made a woman married? Had her husband acted the part of a husband? Had he remained with her? Where was he now, in her time of trial?

He had never been her husband, not as her father had been to her mother. He had been a young man whom she married and with whom, for a time, she lived. And he had left no impression here, not even in his son.

Mentally she stood him before Vittoro, and she saw the old chieftain's decision, understood his scorn. And then she saw Hondo Lane, and he stood squarely before Vittoro, a man.

She worked steadily, yet her thoughts would not remain still. Her problem was with her, and she was a woman born to a Christian life, reared to a moral life, yet always an honest life. Her father had always been a man with whom she could talk, and those talks had reached into her present life with their clear-cut wisdom, their simple truth.

To each of us is given a life. To live with honor and to pass on having left our mark, it is only essential that we do our part, that we leave our children strong. Nothing exists long when its time is past. Wealth is important only to the small of mind. The important thing is to do the best one can with what one has.

These things her father had taught her, these things she believed. A woman's task was to keep a home, to rear her children well, to give them as good a start as possible before moving on. That was why she had stayed. That was why she had dared to remain in the face of Indian trouble. This was her home. This was her fireside. Here was all she could give her son aside from the feeling that he was loved, the training she could give, the education. And she could give him this early belief in stability, in the rightness of belonging somewhere.

Now it was threatened. The very thing that had saved their lives might turn her son from the life that should be his. He was excited by the attentions of the old chief, and he hungered for the company of a man. How else was a boy to learn how to become a man?

Was she a fool to think always of Hondo Lane? The man was a killer.

But this also her father had given her: reserve of judgment, and to judge no man or woman by a grouping, but each on his own character, his own ground.

In Hondo Lane she had recognized some of the same virtues

she had known in her father. The singleness of purpose, the honesty, the steadfastness, and the industry. A killer he might be, but a man must live as he must. There were things a man must face and things a man must do that no woman could understand, just as the reverse was true.

Tonight the hills were lonely. A coyote yapped at the moon, and in the silence a quail called.

How long did she have? How long before Vittoro came again and demanded a decision of her? But Indians did not permit women to make decisions . . . or did they? She had heard not, and yet, knowing women, she was not altogether sure of this. She smiled into the night.

Johnny came out and sat on the steps beside her. "Mommy? Do you think the man will like my headband? Do you think he will?"

"I'm sure of it, Johnny."

Then carefully, thinking of the future, she said, "You're a white boy, Johnny, and although someday you may live with the Indians, you will always be a white boy. Mr. Lane lived with the Indians, and he remained a white man."

Darkness crept in and crouched around the stable, and in the darkness she smelled the sage and heard the stirring and the stamping of the horses in the corral. In the east there was a bright star low above the mountains.

Would he come back again? Would he come in time?

"Mommy!" Johnny pulled at her hand. "What will I have to learn to be a warrior?"

"Oh, you'll have to learn to track wild animals, to ride, to hunt, to find food in the desert . . . many things."

"Will I learn to ride like the man did?"

The man . . . "Yes, I think so." She hesitated just a little. "Maybe he'll come back and teach you. He's a good man, Johnny."

"I liked him." Johnny watched the quiet star. "I liked the dog, too."

"But he snapped at you!"

"But he didn't know me!" Johnny said. "He didn't know I

was his friend! If a dog let anybody touch him before they were friends, somebody might hurt him."

A faint sound caught her ears. She held her breath, listening. It was the sound of a horse . . . of many horses.

And then she saw them, a dozen Indians, filing by toward the spring, just beyond the reach of her light. An Indian's horse's eyes caught the light and reflected it.

An Indian left the group and started toward them. She got to her feet, recognizing Silva.

He stood looking at her, and there was a pride in his bearing, and contempt, too. He gestured at her head, then lifted a scalp at his belt. It was fresh, red-haired.

Another Indian came up behind him and said something. Silva hesitated, looking from her to the child. The other Indian spoke again, more urgently. The only word she knew was "Vittoro." The second Indian used the name several times. Silva turned away, finally, and walked back to the horses.

She stood very still, holding Johnny tightly to her until she heard their horses moving away.

For a long time after they were gone, she was uneasy. Inside she checked the pistol again. Since Hondo had loaded it, and since Johnny had nearly killed Silva, she always kept it loaded.

Silva would come back. He would come alone. Afterward he could always blame some other Indians for what was done. He had forgotten nothing, and he would not forget. Her only hope was to have a man of her own. But who could stand against Silva if anything happened to Vittoro?

She asked the question into the night, and her heart gave her the answer.

TEN

B ehind the stables the lineback was saddled and ready. Hondo Lane came around the corner carrying his rifle. He slid the Winchester into the boot and began tying his bedroll behind the cantle.

He looked over his shoulder when he heard the approaching feet, his fingers continuing to work. It was Ed Lowe, and with him was Sergeant Young.

"See?" Lowe said angrily. "It's my horse. That's my brand."

He indicated the E L on the horse's shoulder. Sergeant Mike Young examined the brand as if hoping to find it a mistake.

He looked up at Hondo. "What he says true?"

"Yes, this is his horse."

"Where did you get it from?"

Hondo looked at Lowe with casual contempt. "From his place. That's where I'm takin' it back. That's where he can find it."

Young hesitated. He liked no part of this. He had no use for Ed Lowe. He knew he was a fourflusher, although a dangerous one. By the same token, he liked Hondo Lane and had ridden in several long patrols guided by Lane. He knew the man and knew him well.

He also knew he had inadvertently walked into something of which he would have preferred to know nothing. There was a standing order that no one was to leave the camp, but at the same time Lane was very close to Major Sherry, and had talked with Sherry on the previous day. The order had gone around that no one was to leave, but at the same time the whisper had followed that no one was to pay any attention to the activities of Hondo Lane. And this had come from the sergeant major.

Major Sherry disciplined his men with strictness, and he had company punishment and the court-martial to enforce it. The sergeant major had only two large fists, but a way of being convincing with them.

Carefully, and merely for the record, Sergeant Young said, "But that's in Injun territory now—strict orders against any white goin' in."

Hondo pulled at his ear. "Know somethin'? I got a bad ear. Can't hear what you're sayin'."

Coolly he stepped into the leather, and then he swung the horse and, keeping the stable between himself and the parade ground, he rode off.

Lowe grabbed the Sergeant's arm. "You can't let him steal my horse!"

Young jerked his arm free. "He may be an ornery son-of-a-anything-you-want-to-call-him, but I'm not calling him a horse thief either to his face or behind his back."

Abruptly Young turned and walked away, glad to be out of it. Behind him he heard Lowe swearing. As Young crossed to his quarters he saw Phalinger come out of the sutler's store, and Young paused at the door of his tent, waiting. A moment later, Ed Lowe crossed the area and joined Phalinger. The two men talked, then walked away together.

Sergeant Major Joe O'Bierne came out of the tent and glanced sharply at Mike Young. "What's the matter?"

Young jerked his head toward the two, then quietly repeated what had happened.

O'Bierne nodded. "You did right, boy. 'Twas none of our affair."

"They'll follow him, I'm thinkin'."

O'Bierne shrugged. "Then on their own shoulders it'll be." He chuckled. "If the Injuns don't get 'em, Lane will, an' good riddance."

Hondo Lane was moving swiftly, with no idea of those who came behind. He knew exactly what situation he faced. Between the post and its relative security and the basin where lay Lowe's ranch, lay miles of country, wild and desolate, crossed and recrossed by hostile Indians. Rarely did they move in as large parties as those encountered by C Company on that fatal day of the massacre. Rather they traveled in smaller groups of eight to a dozen warriors, and were the more dangerous because of this.

An Apache might be anywhere. This was his country, this heat-baked nightmare of waterless, treeless land, cut by no streams and with few water holes. Dotted with clumps of greasewood and cut by savage arroyos or uplifted ledges of black volcanic rock or sandstone, it was a weird and dangerous country over which to travel.

No man knew better the art of concealment than the Apache. His own hide, his instinctive feeling for terrain, and his ability to live for days with little water and less food made him a fearful antagonist always. Hondo Lane rode into that heat-baked wilderness knowing exactly what lay before him. He had lived with the Apache. He knew his ways and much of his thinking, and he knew better than anyone how small was the chance that Angie Lowe and her Johnny were still alive.

Yet he knew also that the Indian was a creature of whim, and although cruel to his enemies or those he believed were enemies, he could be kind to children. No Apache had ever been known to strike his child. He might beat his wife, but never his child. And the very fact that Angie Lowe was alive this long proved she had been fortunate. She might continue to be so.

He moved now as he had before. He scouted the terrain before him, and only then did he move. He knew much of it, but he did not rely on that knowledge. He kept out of low places, held to the concealment just below ridges, studied every fresh track. He wore nothing that gleamed. The lineback's dun color shaded into the desert as did his own clothing.

With no weapons but his bow and arrows, his lance and war club or knife, the Apache had ruled over this vast area for generations, and when the rifle was introduced, he quickly learned its use and became an adept. Although always lacking ammunition, the Apache became a marksman in many cases second to none.

At noon Hondo rode the lineback into an arroyo and swung down, leading the horse back into the shade of an overhang. Some dead curl-leaf lay in the canyon bottom and he collected it, then a few more sticks, all dry. He ate jerky with hardtack, and drank two cups of coffee hastily made over the fire.

The dry wood made no smoke, and when the coffee was hot, Hondo extinguished the fire and carefully buried the coals, brushing over the surface with a loose branch. He squatted there, finishing his coffee and smoking, letting the heat of the day slip by while the lineback ate of the grass close under the cliff's edge.

Sam lay panting in the shade a few yards off. Hondo leaned back against the wall and dozed. Not until two hours had passed did he move, and then he tightened the cinch on the lineback and stepped into the saddle.

Taking his time, he worked his way out of the arroyo, careful to study the country before moving into the open. All afternoon he traveled on, keeping a steady gait but frequently shifting his trail. Several times he paused, studying his backtrail. A faint dust was visible once. A dust devil? Or was it someone on his trail?

At dusk he was approaching Deadman Water Hole, and he took his time. A mile from the water he crossed the trail of four unshod ponies. The trail was scarcely an hour old. A word to Sam and the dog moved out warily, scouting ahead. Hondo moved up to a place among some rocks where he looked over the approaches to the water hole. There was nothing in sight. And then he saw Sam.

The big mongrel was moving closer, belly down among the rocks. Only the faintest of movements rendered him visible. Hondo waited, his rifle ready to cover the dog if need be, but suddenly the dog lifted himself to his legs, seemed to hesitate, sniffing the wind, and then trotted toward the hole. Relieved, Hondo Lane got a foot into the stirrup and swung his leg over. The lineback, sensing the water, walked eagerly forward.

Deadman was a seep. The water was still but fresh, and Hondo drank, then allowed the horse to drink. Sam's muzzle was already wet. The Apaches had been here, but had not remained long. Hondo mounted again and they moved on. Twice he paused before darkness to study his backtrail. He saw nothing.

Far behind him two horsemen rode out of a gully. Ed Lowe was in the lead, Phalinger close behind. Phalinger was a lean, dark man. He stared at the darkening hills.

"I don't like it, Ed."

Lowe said nothing. He had already come farther than he had intended, but turning back was not part of his plan. He was a good man on a trail, but Phalinger was better. It had taken all their skill to follow Hondo Lane, although the big rider was making no undue effort to conceal his passing.

"He's gettin' deep in Injun territory, and so are we," Phalinger added.

"What you squawkin' for? He's carryin' plenty, and you know it. Besides, he ain't goin' much farther without makin' camp."

Phalinger shrugged. "We never found his camp last night."

"We'll find it this time."

They pushed on, finding an occasional track of the shod horse. Lowe had the added advantage of knowing where Lane was headed. He had said he was returning to the ranch, and Lowe believed him. It was an added reason for continuing. No one at the post must ever learn he had abandoned Angie and his child at the ranch. He would not be allowed to stay around for one minute.

That had been one advantage. At the Pass they knew he was married. At the post they knew nothing of him except that he had a ranch and cattle. He had never mentioned Angie.

At first he had intended to return. It was not Indians that worried him, but the long days at the ranch without company. Nor did he want to work. No sense in that. It was easier to play cards and win money from those that did work. So why be a fool? Besides, he had the ranch and cattle. When the Apaches settled down he'd hire a couple of men to round up the steers and sell them to the Army. The rest he would let run, and in time there would be more cattle. Not being there, he'd lose a few, but longhorns knew how to get along. A longhorn bull would tackle anything that walked. They had been known to whip grizzlies.

He tried to avoid thinking of Angie. The thought of her accusing eyes made him uncomfortable. She was all right, only she had such notions about staying with the ranch. As if they wouldn't be better off in town. And she didn't want him to gamble. He won, didn't he? He grinned a little, thinking of how he won. But she didn't know that, and it was none of her business. Besides, he had worked hard enough for two men while her old man was alive.

"Lots of 'Paches movin'," Phalinger said. "If we don't come up with him tonight, I'm goin' back."

Ed Lowe felt rising anger, but stifled it. Phalinger was no man to fool with, and besides, he wanted his company and his help. Ed Lowe was shrewd enough to know that he would get nowhere tackling Hondo Lane alone. The man's reputation had been acquired the hard way.

"Must be packin' a thousand dollars," Lowe said, urging Phalinger's greed. "Where else we goin' to get that much? Take us to Frisco."

"If we live."

They moved on as evening gathered, more slowly now. They

were only a few miles behind Hondo at Deadman. They found the tracks of his horse there overlying those of the Indians.

"All right," Lowe agreed. "It's tonight or we both go back."

They pushed on. Lowe mopped sweat from his face. He had the feeling they were close, and now that they were drawing near his mouth was growing dry, and he was tense.

Long shadows stretched from the hills, the sun died beyond the mountains behind them, and the air grew cool. Lowe's shirt felt sticky and uncomfortable. Phalinger moved closer. From time to time they paused, listening.

"Ed."

Lowe turned to Phalinger. The gambler's face was white and set.

"I got a hunch, Ed. I got a gambler's hunch. We've had it."

Irritation mounted within Lowe, stifling his own doubt. "Don't be a damn fool!" He kept his voice down. "Hour from now we'll have him right where we want him. It's him ain't goin' to get back."

Their horses walked in sand. Ahead leaves rustled. Leaves meant a cottonwood, and a cottonwood meant water. Ed Lowe's hatred mounted within him. He loosened his gun, urged his horse forward, then stopped.

A faint sound reached him: a hoof on stone, the creak of saddle leather.

Lowe drew back, triumph choking him. "We got him!" he breathed. "Let's move back a bit. We got him right where we want him!"

ELEVEN

When Angie had collected a double handful of the tender stalks of the squaw cabbage she put them in a basket and straightened to look at the hills. They were brown now, the grass fading under the blazing summer heat.

The days had passed slowly, each filled with its quota of work, but days that found her going more and more often to look from her doorstep at the surrounding hills. Hondo had said nothing of returning, and yet within her she was sure he had intended to come back.

Had she really read that intention in him, or was it only that the wish was father to the thought?

And her time was growing short. At any time Vittoro might return and say that she must choose now. Perhaps she should have gone with Hondo when he wanted to take her. She might be with him now. Yet she could not bear to leave all this, this place to which she had given the labor of her hands, and where she had seen her father rebuild the house, and lay the poles for the corral.

A man might drift, but a woman must belong somewhere, if it was no more than a hovel on a hillside. A woman must have a home, and this belonged to her. To herself and to Johnny.

95

There had been a great battle fought. That she knew from the scalps she had seen and the cavalry horses ridden by the Apaches. They had slaughtered one and eaten it not a half mile down the arroyo. Why the Apaches preferred horse and mule meat to good beef she did not know, but so they did, preferring mule meat to all else.

Her father had told her once that the early-day mountain men had liked the meat of the panther best, preferring it to the most tender venison. And they had their choice of game in a country where only Indians had hunted and there was much game.

Picking up her basket, she walked back, going a little out of her way to look at the bushes along the creek. There would be berries later in the season. Maybe enough to preserve some for the winter. This year would be the first when Johnny could help, and anxious as he was to appear a man, she knew he would do more than his share.

She had reached the house and was washing the cabbage stalks when she heard the rush of hoofs. At one moment the ranch was silent and the next it was a circle of rushing horses, a half-dozen hard-riding Indians sweeping by at a dead run, picking objects from the ground, leaping on and off their horses, performing like a circus gone mad.

Rifle in hand, she stopped at the door, staring in consternation at the yelling, charging Indians. Then she saw Vittoro, standing calmly beside the door.

"I thought the Apache were always silent."

"Except during the squaw-seeking ceremony."

Angie felt her heart miss a beat. For an instant she held herself still. "The what?"

"Ceremony of seeking new squaw. Then the braves show off their skill that the squaw may choose."

He took a step forward and lifted a hand. "Hola!"

The Indians swung into a charging line and rode up, rearing their horses, then quieting them to sit waiting.

"You will pick one. It is not good for Small Warrior to grow up without a father to teach him how to perform a man's duty."

Fascinated, she stared at Vittoro, and then at the Indians. Physically, they were magnificent specimens. Two were tall, the others the barrel-chested men of medium height typical of the Apaches. All were dressed in their fanciest regalia, but at least two wore parts of uniforms taken from dead soldiers.

Vittoro gestured at the one on the left. "This is the one called Emiliano. Very brave, and has six horses. Two squaws, but one is old and will soon be gone. He is a good hunter. It is never hungry where he sits.

"This one is Kloori. Ten horses, only one squaw. He is . . ."

Turning swiftly, Angie ran into the house, her heart throbbing painfully, too frightened almost to breathe. As she fought to regain control, tears came into her eyes. She heard Vittoro come into the house behind her, and turned quickly to face him.

Turning to Johnny, he said, "Go stand by my horse."

"Yes, Vittoro."

When the boy had gone the old Indian said sternly, "Small Warrior is never to see tears. The Apache does not weep."

Angie drew herself up. Desperation gave her strength. "Chief, you can't make me . . . I'm married."

"Married? Oh, the white man's word for it. You are a fool. Your man is dead."

"No. I do not know he is dead. Among my people it is not so easy. I . . . I must be sure. But even if it were true, I don't know . . . I . . ."

Vittoro did not seem to be listening. He gestured toward the waiting braves. "Sachito. Brave warrior. Many horses, does not beat squaws much. Sings very loud."

Desperately she searched for an argument that might move him, some common ground. Suddenly she believed she had it. "You don't understand. It would be against my religion. You Apaches have your own religion, and live up to it. I know that. Can't you understand? Can't you see that if mine tells me—"

Vittoro was impatient. He spoke quickly now, and more sharply. He was not accustomed to arguing with women, and the warriors who waited outside were the pride of his people, not to be lightly disdained by any woman.

"When religion makes you act like a fool, it is a wrong religion." He hesitated, then said brusquely, "Very well! I have decided. We will wait." He pointed toward the mountains. "Soon will come the planting rain. If your man comes by then, good. If not, you take Apache brave. It is spoken."

He walked out of the house without a backward glance, mounted his pony, and, followed by the braves, rode from the basin. Angie, her heart pounding, watched them go.

Again, for a little while, she was safe. And after that there would be no choice. For a few minutes she thought of flight, suddenly, and in the night. Then she knew the absurdity of the idea, for by daylight they would be upon her trail and then there would be no more waiting . . . if they did not kill her out of hand. And one among them, at least, would do just that. She remembered the hatred in the eyes of Silva.

There would be no chance to get away, for she knew what an Apache on a trail was like, and she knew nothing of hiding a trail, and with Johnny they could not travel fast. She was not even sure exactly where the Army post lay. And even there she might not find security. Who knew if there was even an Army post left? Many soldiers had been killed, perhaps all of them.

Yet from that moment she began to plan. There was no definite knowledge of what Hondo planned to do. She was foolish to think he might return, and the chance that Ed might return was even smaller. She must now, as always, rely upon herself.

The thing to do was to remain quiet, yet to plan and make preparations. She would need two horses, she would need food and ammunition. She did not know exactly where the post lay, yet she did know where the Pass was, and the Pass was large enough to be safe from any Indian attack. There was an Army post there, also, and there were rangers there.

Somewhere among her father's things there was a map—she remembered seeing him make it—and if she could find it, she might be able to plan a way out. And he had taught her, while she was only a little girl, to use the stars to guide her travel. There would be a time when the braves of Vittoro would be far away at battle, raiding in Mexico or elsewhere. She had learned to know those times, and often the parties went through her basin on their way out.

The next time they went, she would take her horses and go at once, within the hour.

That night, after Johnny was asleep, she packed the saddlebags with ammunition and filled two canteens. If she had to wait she could always refill them. She prepared some jerky, placed it and some hardtack where they could be reached and packed in an instant.

Searching through her father's trunk, she found the map. It was a square of some twenty inches of hide, the lines drawn and notations made in his painstaking hand. The map itself was not crude, but a small work of art. She located the ranch, then searched out a way among the buttes and canyons by which they could travel.

Only one of the horses was fit to ride, so she must break the other. Fortunately, she believed, there would be time. If there was not, she could always take Johnny on the same horse. Yet she went at once to the corral and remained beside the horses until it was completely dark, talking to them and feeding them.

She could not conquer them as Hondo had done, but the horse she needed was a much less dangerous animal, and she had seen both her father and Hondo make friends with a horse until the battle was half won. Those were the tactics she would use; they were all that remained to her.

Once her decision was made, she planned every move with it in mind. There was an old lock. . . . Perhaps the Indians would break it, but she could at least try to protect her house until she returned.

She would wait until every other chance was gone. Perhaps she might escape during the rain. With the rain to wipe out her tracks, their chances would be greater. Yet that meant exposing Johnny to the fury of the storm . . . for storm it would be when the planting rain came.

It was almost midnight before Angie finally retired. During most of that time she had tried to plan her course of action. At the last moment she might have to act entirely opposite to her decided course, but she would have a plan. What to do would depend upon the events of the moment, but the very fact that she had a plan gave her confidence and a feeling of greater security.

Yet even as her eyes closed, her last conscious thought was that Hondo Lane might return. And the question remained in her mind: What had happened between them that she should feel so sure of how he felt? So little had been said, so little done. Yet the knowledge was there, and a deep inner realization that this was the man with whom she could be happy, this was the man with whom she wanted to live out her years.

And it could never be. Even if she escaped the Indians, if she survived all the fighting, and if Hondo felt about her as she felt about him, there was still no chance for happiness for either of them. There was always Ed Lowe. He might be dead, but Angie was not prepared to believe that. And he was her husband, the father of her child.

At daybreak an idea came to her. The Apaches would know how many horses were in the corral, and when two were missing they would immediately know she had fled. But for that she could plan. That very morning she led out two of the horses and picketed them on the grass in the trees and out of sight of any passing Indians. She would do this occasionally, while still remaining in sight herself. In that way the Indians would not be suspicious when they noticed the missing horses. There were several places they could be picketed out of sight, and where they could not be found without a search. Thus their disappearance would not be sudden, and not a cause for investigation.

Yet even as she worked and planned, Angie knew that her chances of escape were small. Only one thing made her decision to make the attempt one from which she could not retreat. There was no other way.

She was hanging out her wash when she heard approaching

horses. Turning quickly, she saw that three Indians had ridden their ponies into the ranch yard. Scarcely two hours after the horses had been moved, and the Indians were here!

One of them was Silva.

They rode around the corral, noting the tracks. One of them rode in the direction the horses had gone, then returned, saying something to Silva. He shrugged, then walked his pony toward Angie.

She faced him, standing very straight, her face composed. To show terror could mean death, and she knew that of them all, Silva feared Vittoro less than the rest. He was, she knew, some sort of subchief.

"What do you want?"

He looked at her insolently. "Maybe soon you be my squaw."

"You?" Her contempt was plain. "Of all the braves in the lodges of the Apache, you would be the last, Fighter of Women!"

Silva's nostrils flared and temper quickened his eyes. It would not do to tempt this man too far, she realized. His was a hair-trigger temper, and he was naturally vindictive. Nor had he forgotten his defeat by her child. The story must have aroused many a chuckle in the wickiups.

One of the two braves riding with him was Emiliano. She remembered him instantly as one of those who had come with Vittoro to the squaw-seeking ceremony. He was a lean and powerful Indian, not the sort to be intimidated.

"I no fight women!" Silva's temper lashed at her. "I kill soldier! I count plenty coups!"

Sensing sympathy from the other Indians, she answered him. "And my child counted coup over you, Brave Warrior! And he is but six summers! Think, Brave Warrior!" Her contempt was thick. "What if he had been twelve?"

Silva started forward as if prodded with a lance, but Emiliano's voice rang sharply.

Silva whirled his horse and the two Indians faced each other, tempers flaring. The third Apache looked at her and she thought she detected a faint smile on his face. Whatever was said

between Silva and Emiliano, the former suddenly wheeled his
horse, and moved away.

The others hesitated a moment, and then Angie said quietly,
"Thank you, Emiliano. I shall speak of this to Vittoro."

His eyes held her briefly, then the two wheeled their ponies
and followed after Silva. It was only then that reaction set in.
What if Emiliano had not been there? What if Silva had with
him some braves more of his own nature?

He would never, she knew instinctively, make this mistake
again.

Suddenly her knees began to tremble, and the muscles in
her legs shook uncontrollably. She got to the house and sat
down on the steps, and it was a long time before she could
move.

She had been a fool to stay on. She had been a silly fool.
What good would she be to her son if they were taken to an
Indian village? What good would the ranch be to either of
them?

She would think no more of Hondo Lane. She would not
think of Ed. Neither of them would come. The latter was
faithless and vacillating, the former had no reason to return.
No real reason. She was a lonely woman and her loneliness had
magnified his respect and a chance kiss into something that was
not there.

She would think of one thing only: escape. When the planting rain came, she would go. And if the rains were hard, they
would wash out her tracks, and she would take a direction
where they would never expect her. Then she might escape.

In the night she was awakened suddenly. A waiting moment
of silence, then a sudden rush of hoofs across the hard-packed
yard, then a hoarse cry. A long moment when there was no
sound, then a shot and after it a long-drawn, wailing scream as
of a mortal soul in pain.

Crouching by the window, rifle in hand, she peered out, and
she could see nothing, only the moonlight on the cottonwood
leaves, only the white-seeming roof of the stable, only the
empty hills.

A dream? No. Johnny was crouching beside her, trembling, partly from cold and partly fear. He tugged at her arm. "Mommy! Mommy, what was that? What happened? Did the man come back?"

Did the man come back?

She felt something like horror mounting within her. Had he come back and been killed at her door?

There was no more sleep. When Johnny was safely in bed she wrapped a blanket about her and sat by the window, the rifle at her hand.

Slowly, with a quiet chill, the night passed. A faint yellow faded the eastern sky, the tips of the cottonwoods turned gold, like the sun-tipped lances of a moving army. The shadows in the yard drew back, hiding in the barn and under the brush along the stream, crouching there. A quail sent out an inquiring call, and somewhere across the basin another quail responded.

It was morning.

TWELVE

When Phalinger and Ed Lowe had ridden back a quarter of a mile from Hondo's place of stopping, Lowe drew up. "Look," he said quietly. "We've got him. Right now he's makin' camp. He'll be mighty cautious. So we let him be. Come daylight, either before he's up or when he's gettin' up, we'll take him."

The gambler shrugged. "Your party." He studied the hills.

"His fingers will be stiff then."

Phalinger looked at Lowe with a faint shadowing of contempt. "Don't take many chances, do you?"

"Why be a sucker?"

From the position Lowe had chosen, the arroyo was in view. They could not see Hondo Lane, nor could he see them, but escape from his camp was impossible without alerting them.

Phalinger was quiet. The farther he had gone, the less he liked any part of it. He was a man without qualms. Lowe knew little about him aside from his utter lack of scruples and the fact that he was a slick second-dealer who knew cards and who worked well with a partner. Phalinger had done murder in Missouri, drifted west into Kansas, then south into Texas. He was wanted in both places.

Yet he had an admiration for a brave man, and Hondo Lane was such a man. Despite the fact that he worked with Lowe, he despised him. Yet not even Phalinger knew that Lowe had deserted a woman in Indian country. Had he known, he might have killed him out of hand.

Phalinger was restless. Their camp was good. They needed no fire. They had food and whisky. Nevertheless, the premonition he had felt earlier now returned. Hondo Lane was carrying several months' wages from the Army and a small poke of gold of his own. It would make a rich haul, and gambling had not been profitable. Too many had lost to them and the word had gone around. It was time to drift, and without money drifting was impossible.

Broodingly he watched Lowe. What drove the man? What was there in him aside from greed and hatred? Yet no man was all bad. Phalinger, who was bad in most ways, knew that he himself was not all bad. Lying on his back he looked up at the stars, thinking about Lowe. He decided that Lowe was weak . . . weak and jealous.

He would always, Phalinger decided, strike at what was stronger and better than himself.

The only reason that Lowe had neither left him nor struck at him, the gambler was sure, was because he considered himself smarter or braver. The thought was galling.

"It better be tomorrow." He said the words suddenly. "I'm going back."

"It'll be tomorrow."

Hondo Lane had made dry camp in the gully. It was also a camp without fire. He was drawing too near to his objective now to take any chances. Also, there had been occasional dust along his backtrail, and once his eye had caught a flash of sunlight on some moving object behind him.

He could be mistaken, of course. But somebody seemed to be trailing him—somebody not an Indian.

The bed he had chosen was in a small open space in the middle of a thicket of mountain mahogany and prickly pear. There was a little catclaw, too. In this place he could sleep without fear, for nothing human could approach his bed without making considerable noise.

On the soft sand he hollowed a place for his hips and rolled in his blankets and ground sheet. He slept, as always, gun in hand.

His saddle lay beside him, his rifle in the scabbard, and his horse was picketed a few feet away. Sam crept under the brush on his belly and put his dark muzzle down on his paws and looked at the man he loved.

The man had strange ways, but he was Sam's friend, and they understood each other. And upon this night Sam too was restless. Twice that day his nostrils had caught a vague smell, faintly familiar, but scarcely tangible. Sam was uneasy, no more.

A quarter of a mile apart three men looked at the night sky. One was discontented with his situation, but ready to accept the profits of murder; the second was thinking first of murder and second of profit; and the third, lying on the sand among the thorns and brush, thought of a cabin, of the firelight on a woman's face, and of her shadow on the wall as he tried to go to sleep.

The moving shadow of a woman on a wall, and the faint sounds of a woman working. It had been a long time, a long, lonely, restless time, since he had heard such sounds.

The lineback had found some grass. He pulled at it, then ate. The sound of his moving jaws was pleasantly relaxing. The man who thought of a woman went to sleep.

Twice in the night the dog awakened and looked at the man, then listened with pricked ears. Had he heard something, far off? He listened and the night listened around him, and there was no sound, and the dark muzzle lowered to the paws against the sand, and the dog's eyes closed, and the horse, too, lay down.

A coyote moved to the arroyo's edge and lifted his nose to

the sky, but catching the scent of dog and man, it moved warily away.

Three miles to the south and west a Mescalero walked up a trail, then suddenly stopped. His feet, sensitive through the moccasins, detected something wrong in the path. He knelt, his fingers explored, and he found the indentation made by a horseshoe.

He muttered something to the others, who gathered around him, and the three stood talking in undertones and looking away to the north and east. Then they walked their horses into a hollow hand of hills and prepared to wait until morning.

There was a white man ahead of them, and possibly more than one. These were scalps to be had, coups to be counted, and they would return to their village men made stronger by the death of enemies. Their dark faces relaxed and they did not talk. And then they, too, went to sleep.

And the planet turned slowly in the vast night sky, and the stars looked down, and there was a smell of damp and coolness in the air. Far over the mountains low clouds gathered. Perhaps the planting rain?

Under a quiet sky the planet turned, and horses ate, and men slept, and death waited for morning.

A bright star hung like a distant lamp in the sky when Hondo opened his eyes. He did not lie still. To awaken was to rise, and he did so now, getting swiftly to his feet, buckling on his gun belt, holstering the gun, and drawing on his boots.

Sam came to his feet with one swift, unnoticed motion as Hondo rolled his bed. The dog growled low, and Hondo looked up at him, watching.

The Indians were near, and their moving disturbed a rattler, which coiled and sent out a short, sharp warning. Hondo relaxed, but Sam growled.

"Cut it out, Sam! I can hear him."

Yet in that instant, his perceptions sharpened by danger, he sensed something else. The dog was disturbed as he had not seen him before, and the dog was not directing his attention toward the sound of the rattler.

There was a frozen instant when Hondo's ears caught at sound, when with the instincts of a wild thing he dropped suddenly and rolled over the bank beneath its added protection, backed by the deeper portion of the brush-choked gully. As he moved, one swift grab slid the Winchester into his hands.

And after that single, violent, animal-like dive for safety, all was still, unmoving. And the movement itself had been relatively soundless.

Now Hondo lay still, listening, scarcely able to breathe. A bee buzzed near, landed on a bush. Hondo could see the texture of the wings, the flexing of the tiny muscles of the body. Sam was quiet. The lineback, seemingly aware of the sudden tension, was still. Not a sound disturbed the clear, bell-like beauty of the morning. There was nothing.

And then there was.

Two riders showed up suddenly on the canyon rim, rifles ready, starkly outlined against the morning.

Lowe and Phalinger had ridden their horses forward through soft sand. At first they considered crawling to the rim, but Lowe was aware of the dog's danger, and had no desire to come upon the big mongrel suddenly. It would be a simple matter to ride right up to the rim, keeping a spacing of about twenty yards, then fire. Hondo Lane would be offered two shots, which was sure to make him hesitate an instant if he saw them at all, and they could cut him down.

The plan was perfect—up to a point. They had not counted on the alertness of Hondo Lane or the hearing of Sam.

Nor did they know about the Apaches.

Phalinger liked no part of it. His heart was pounding and his mouth was dry. He had no breakfast, and he desperately wanted coffee. They had killed their whisky during the long night and his nerves were jumpy. It was too quiet. Moreover, he was moved by the beauty of the morning. Something deep within him seemed urging him to stop, to breathe, to enjoy.

This was something one could not buy in bottles. It was bright, clear, all too beautiful.

Phalinger had killed. He had shot men in the back, and he would not hesitate to do so again. Yet he loved life and loved it dearly, and in that awful moment of realization he saw in the clear, sharp beauty of the morning what wasted years he had left behind. He looked over at Lowe, started to speak.

And he hesitated. Lowe was alert, tense. His rifle was ready. Lowe was a killer, as are many cowardly things, and he could not accept that there should live things and persons superior to him. Angie's father had always been a better man, but wanting the ranch, Ed Lowe had played a game, fooling the father more successfully than he could ever fool the daughter.

Their horses walked in the soft earth. They moved forward, step by step. Before them their view of the arroyo widened, the morning grew brighter. The sun lay against the far bank and at their backs, for they had circled for this advantage, so that Hondo would have to fire into the glare of the sun.

Phalinger heard a bird call. He heard the soft fall of his horse's hoofs. A leaf brushed his face, and off across the far hills there were low clouds. The very canyons, moraines, and hanging valleys showed sharply clear in the bright air. He liked the feel of the horse moving under him, liked the smell of it. He liked the smell of sage, and of crushed cedar. . . . Why had he waited so long to realize this?

Lowe caught his eye with a signal. Phalinger's rifle came up. It was live or die now. They breasted the slope.

They saw the rolled blankets, the open space in the brush, the linebacked horse . . . and nothing else!

In that single, awful moment of awareness, both men were caught, suspended, in the moment. Both had expected a target, were ready for it . . . and there was nothing.

Then from Phalinger's far right a flash of sunlight on a rifle barrel turned his head. For one swift, stark moment he saw the Apache, saw the dark, slim body, saw the rifle muzzle not forty yards away, and knew he looked upon death.

He lifted his rifle, and heard soft, gasping words torn from him. "Oh, God!" And then the rifle bullet smashed into his jaw, tearing through his throat, and he fell.

His horse sprang from under him. Vaguely he heard other shots, but they were not for him, nor was he for them. He lay flat on his face with the taste of blood and earth in his mouth and he was choking and he was seeing again the bright morning he had left, and with his last muscular effort he rolled over to look at the sky.

There was a white cloud there, so small, so lonely, so white against the vast blue dome of the morning. For day had come. It was here, and Phalinger looked up at the sky and saw the cloud fade and knew he was gone and he tried to speak past the blood and there were no words, there was nothing any more. . . .

One moment there had been nothing and then the two riders appeared on the skyline. Their wide separation rang a bell of warning in Hondo's brain, but at the same time he knew that while it was this that had disturbed Sam, it was not this that had disturbed the rattler. And the crash of shots told him he was right.

He saw the nearer man drop, saw him hit the ground, heard a thin, despairing cry. Then he saw the other man drop also.

The Apaches had been following Hondo Lane. They had not expected two men. They had no reason to believe there could be three.

To count coup upon the body of a dead enemy is not so great a glory as to do it upon a living one. All three Apaches sprang suddenly forward . . . into death.

The nearest Apache was a tall, splendidly built man, and he sprang eagerly, rifle held high. Hondo Lane's bullet took him under the breastbone, striking at an angle, and ripped out of his side below the heart. The splendid leap was the last movement, for when the Apache touched the ground all that amazing wiry strength was dead, a blasted, wasted thing, giving blood to the sand.

Hondo fired swiftly, saw the second man go down, the third vanish.

For an instant Hondo lay still. The second white man to be shot by the Apaches had fallen from his horse into the arroyo. Worming his way through the brush, Hondo made it to his side. It was Ed Lowe.

Even as he reached his side and laid down his rifle, the remaining warrior leaped from the brush into the saddle of Phalinger's horse and was gone from sight.

Hondo checked Lowe, then sat back on his heels. "You're not hurt too bad."

Lowe, badly shaken, sat up. Some color was returning to his face. There was blood on his shirt. He drew a picture from his shirt pocket. "This tintype saved me."

The bullet had struck his chest at a flat angle and, hitting the tintype, had glanced away, tearing the skin beyond it with a burn rather than a wound.

Hondo Lane got to his feet, picking up his rifle. "I wish that Indian hadn't got away. All the Apaches between here and the post will be alerted now."

"You mean we're cut off?"

"What else?" Lane turned to study the terrain carefully. It was time to move. No telling how far away there were other Indians.

As Lane turned away, Ed Lowe realized two things: Here was the man he had come to kill, and there was only one horse left—Lane's horse.

Hondo heard the sudden sharp growl from Sam. He side-stepped quickly as he turned and saw the flash of Lowe's gun. Hondo fired his rifle from the hip and the bullet smashed Ed Lowe back to the sand. His muscles convulsed, bringing him almost erect. Hondo Lane did not fire again.

Lowe came almost up, then fell, and there was no sound in the brightness of the desert morning.

Hondo looked down at what had been Angie's husband, then picked up the tintype. It was a picture of Johnny.

He dropped to the sand, his face gray and ghastly, holding the tintype and his rifle and realization. And Sam came close and nudged against him, whining softly. And this time he was allowed to come close.

THIRTEEN

For an hour of lonely riding there had been no life upon the desert. The sun was high, and sweat trickled down Hondo's neck, and the body of the lineback became dark with stain. And before them stretched the vast and rolling plain of sand, rock, and cactus that is the desert of the Southwest.

Here there was no moment of security. Somewhere out there the escaped Apache had joined his friends, and somewhere those hard and tireless desert fighters were moving out, beginning their search for him.

Desert . . . but a desert strangely alive. Not a dead land, but a land where all life is born with a fire, a thorn, a sting. Yet a strong land, a rich land for the man who knows it. One cannot fight the desert and live. One lives with it, or one dies. One learns its way and its life, and moves with care, and never ceases to be wary, for the desert has traps and tricks for the careless.

The lineback walked with dainty feet, knowing this land, knowing its fears and its dangers. And on his back Hondo Lane never ceased to watch, taking in each small shadow, each dark rock, each possible place of cover before moving on. Once, riding along a rocky hillside, he followed the fresh trail of a

112

deer. Suddenly the animal's tracks broke sharply to the left and into the bottom.

Hondo swung the lineback and followed, his hand ready for his rifle. Whatever the deer had seen or heard might now be gone, but he was not gambling. Later he came upon the fresh trail of a mountain lion. Probably not Apaches, then.

He followed down the arroyo until it widened into a small valley where a stream flowed, cottonwood and willow lining its banks. Riding into the brush, he dismounted. Then, slipping off his boots, he walked back, brushing out his trail and leaving the tracks pointed toward the water as if to ride in or cross the stream.

Then he retreated carefully, avoiding branches. Wild game will not step on fallen branches. Neither would an Indian. Only a horse, a cow, or a white man would be so foolish. The weight of the horse or cow or man would break the branch into finer pieces and press it into the ground. Hondo retreated with care, and when he was in the shelter of the trees he loosened the girth on the saddle and sat down with his back against a tree.

It was not yet noon, at least an hour short of it, but the heat was great despite the time of year, and he must conserve both his horse's strength and his own. He chewed on some jerky and hardtack while the horse cropped grass, then went down to the stream through the thick brush and drank. Then he emptied his canteen and refilled it with cold, fresh water.

After an hour's rest he pulled on his boots and tightened the girth. At the edge of the small grove where he had waited, he studied the terrain with care before moving out. Knowing the Apaches, he had no idea they would lose his trail. All he could do would be to delay their pursuit as much as possible. Yet now, when he left the grove, he rode swiftly forward, following down the stream bed, using the concealment of its trees. He left the creek on a shelf of rock and rode straight up the side of the valley. The last few feet was a hard scramble, but they topped the crest and were immediately off the ridge.

A wide, long valley opened before him, dotted with the tall sentinel fingers of saguaro and the serrated ridge of an upthrust ledge that cut down the opposite wall. It was of dark, sun-blackened rock. The lineback was rested and he moved out eagerly.

Suddenly a startled bird flew up some distance off, and instantly Hondo swung the lineback. The Apaches broke into sight scarcely seconds later, but the lineback was already running. With wild, shrill yells the Indians booted their ponies and the chase was on.

The lineback was a fast, powerful animal with fire and a love of running. He took to it now, mane flying, nose into the wind.

Glancing back, Hondo saw he was gaining ground, and suddenly he heard a whining yelp from Sam, and turning back he saw four more Indians coming down off the ridge ahead of him. To turn to avoid them was to lose distance, but there was no help for it. He swung the racing horse into a branching canyon and went up the side on a long angle.

There were at least eight Apaches behind him now, and they had gained ground. He went up the ridge and then suddenly before him there was a long gray slide of shale. There was no stopping. The lineback plunged into it, lost footing and went down. Sam was racing close and he was lost in the swirl of dust. The horse scrambled madly, fighting for a foothold, got it, and Hondo went back into the saddle and then he saw Sam come out of the dust on three legs.

With a quick glance back at the Indians, Hondo bent and scooped the injured dog into his arms, and then they were racing away again.

The time lost was too much. The Apaches had gained, and even as he cleared the ridge they converged around him. There was no chance to grab a gun with the dog in his arms, and they sprang from their horses and knocked him from the saddle. He struck out viciously, the dog leaped away, snapping at Silva, who was one of the attackers, but then the Indians were all over him.

Hondo Lane was thrown on his face and his hands were jerked behind him and lashed hard with rawhide.

A few yards away Sam stood, growling, waiting the expected

command to attack. It was not given. Hondo glanced around.
Nine Indians.

Silva's eyes went to Sam, and he turned and barked a re-
quest at the nearest warrior for his bow and an arrow.

Hondo jerked his head around. "Sam! Vete, Sam! Vete!"

Instantly the big dog wheeled and darted into the brush,
making fast time even with his bad leg. Once back in the brush
he crouched and crawled back, lying in the brush, growling
low in his chest, but securely out of sight.

Silva walked to Hondo and struck him across the face. There
was cold triumph in his eyes. There would be a big time in the
village this night. This man was strong. If he had courage, he
might live a long time. . . . But why delay? Why wait until
night? He could sing of his deeds when they returned, and the
man was here, now.

"The white man speaks our language," he said. "It is good.
He will know his treatment in advance."

"Your coup stick shows many scalps."

"Truly."

Hondo spoke slowly, clearly, and with contempt thick upon
the words. He knew the Apache, knew the words would lash
his fury. "You took them from squaws and papooses and dogs.
Your lodge should be proud of you."

Hondo spoke in Spanish, then in the tongue of the Apache.
One of the Indians gave a grunt of laughter, but Silva's eyes
flared hot and ugly. The insult had not been expected.

"Truly," the Apache said, "you will feel much."

"It is nothing," Hondo sneered, "to torture a captured man.
You are a woman of the village, a runner after rabbits. Without
the bravery of these others you would be food for coyotes
now!"

Hondo Lane spoke with cold calculation. He was a man who
knew his land, and knew the people who held him now. There
was always, one thought, a chance of escape. Rarely with the
Apache. He bound his captives too brutally, he stayed with
them too closely. A prisoner had only to die . . . to die slowly,
over a fire, head down, or staked out on an ant hill, or bound

in a green hide and laid out in the hot sun. Or one might die quickly. If Silva could be angered enough . . .

But Silva was a patient as well as a vindictive man. There was no desire in him to give the white man quick death instead of the hours of torture he planned. And this one had courage. He was a strong man, with wiry, powerful muscles. He would die slowly, and when at the end he broke, it would be a triumph to be remembered.

Silva's anger at the insults was a white-hot thing that wound through his body like blazing wire. But the man was here, tied, a prisoner. A delayed revenge could be the sweeter for all of that. And when they tied Hondo Lane upon a horse, his hands were bound so tightly that they swelled. And then they moved on, winding across the long hills, a tiny cavalcade of Apaches, barebacked on their ponies, their flat faces emotionless and still.

And with the afternoon the heat became a living thing. The sun hung in a wide sky and seemed to spread until all the sky was a great reflector pouring its heat upon the desert, which reflected it back. And the vast distance was a space across which moved the tiny figures of the Apaches and their captive, and sitting his horse, Hondo Lane lost himself in a world of pain and heat and movement where there was only feeling and where all was lost in space and there was no time. . . .

The moments became hours and the hours weeks and the days seemed years. His hands had swollen greatly, his shirt was soaked with sweat, and the salt sweat got into his eyes and they smarted, red-rimmed and narrowed against the sun and the glare.

Yet behind the monotony of their travel, behind the blank vacancy of his face where lay a world sodden with pain, behind it all there still prowled the restless desperation of a strong man wanting to live. There was no way now . . . but there might be a way.

Bitter within him was the desire to fight, to die in battle if no more, but to escape, to get away, to live. The bitterness of his capture was through him like a poison. He stared through heat-rimmed eyes at the evil face of Silva, knowing instinct-ively that here was his enemy. This one was the one he must kill.

The distance shimmered with heat. Sweat trickled down his body under his shirt. He felt the pain in his hands and the wicked bite of the taut rawhide, cutting into the raw flesh.

And he lifted his head and stared at Silva. He spat. "Squaw!" he sneered. His hatred made his speech ugly. "Old woman!"

Silva's head turned, his eyes liquid with ugliness. Then the Indian looked ahead once more.

Hondo Lane was tempted to touch a spur to the lineback, to lunge into the Indian, to make a break for it, hands tied or not. But his good sense told him the futility of that. There would be a time. He must wait. He flexed his stiff, swollen fingers. But he made no sound. He did not groan, he did not curse.

At every step of the horse his hands hurt him, at every move there was new pain.

He hung his head forward and let his body move with the steps of the lineback, and his mind lost itself in remembering. The ranch beside the stream, the clear, cold water, the woman with the clear, expressive eyes, her quiet movements about the house, and the sound of a child's voice . . . A yearning mounted within him and the pain was forgotten. He remembered the dry rustle of the cottonwood leaves, the good taste of coffee, the smell of wood smoke from her fireplace.

Then he smelled smoke, and another, older, more familiar smell. An Apache *rancheria*.

He looked up and saw them. It was familiar, old in his memory, the sights, the smells. He almost looked for the quick movement of Destarte. But she was gone, dead.

He saw the flat, hard faces of the men, the wide cheekbones, the square jaws, the headbands.

How many times had he come here from hunting to such a place? How many months had he lived among such people as these? There might be some here who knew him. There might be those with whom he had hunted, and with whom he had ridden to Mexico to steal horses for their people.

He sat straight in the saddle, holding his head up, looking neither to right nor to left. If he must die, he would show them how a man should go, he would show them with contempt and insults that there burned within him a fire that could not die. He knew the Apache heart, knew the Apache mind.

When they stopped he looked around him at the brown faces, saw the one man who stood apart and knew it.

Hondo Lane said loudly, "It is my shame that I am taken by warriors with whom rides an old woman."

Hondo was taken roughly from the saddle and the rawhide was cut from his hands. He was shoved into position beside the fire. There was a pot of water standing there, and without asking questions he dipped his swollen hands into it, feeling the coolness of the water soothing the pain.

Vittoro, who had stood aside, came to the circle around the fire and looked down at him.

"The white man speaks our language," Silva said. "He has spoken many insults."

FOURTEEN

H ondo gently chafed his hands. Nobody had made any move to stop him from administering to his hands. He glanced up to see Vittoro studying him. The old chief acknowledged Silva's remark.

"It is a brave man who insults at such a moment." To Hondo he said suddenly, "Where are the pony soldiers, white man? And how many are they?"

"This I do not know, Vittoro."

"You know how I am called?"

"I saw you at the treaty council at Fort Meade."

"The treaty! The rustle of wind to the white man." His voice grew sharper. "Where are the pony soldiers?"

"This I do not know."

Vittoro gestured toward the saddle on the lineback. "Your saddle bears the mark of the pony soldier."

"Once I was a pony soldier. Now I am not."

Vittoro seated himself and looked across the corner of the fire at Hondo's swollen hands. They looked bad, but already they felt better. The swelling had been caused by the tight binding, and once they were released, much of the swelling had gone down.

119

"If you are not a spy, what do you seek in our land?"

Hondo Lane hesitated, and then he said more slowly, careful to make his voice sound its respect, "This is for me to know, Chief. What I do does no harm to the people of Vittoro, or to any Apache."

Vittoro got to his feet and walked away across the camp. And then for a time Hondo was left alone. His feet were tied but his hands were free. He flexed their muscles, feeling the swelling going away. His wrists were lacerated by the tight-drawn rawhide, but the blood was flowing normally once more.

He looked around him at the *rancheria* in the shallow valley. It was a scene anciently familiar to him . . . the low wickiups of brush or hides gathered about pyramided sticks, the horses grazing, the children playing about.

Only then he had not been a prisoner. He had been one of them. An alien, yes, but a friend and a hunting companion and the man of Destarte. And he smelled the desert air, the smell of roasting venison and mule meat, the nopal drying and watched the people moving about their tasks.

He sat alone. Knowing the ways of these people, he knew the death that awaited him now, knew what they would do, and knew that he must be strong, to show no fear, to show no pain. He must at all costs die well.

And it was not so easy to die well. He had seen other men die, and he had seen the remains of men who had died well. It had never seemed possible that what they had endured could be endured by any man. Could he do as well?

A squaw brought him food, and he thanked her in her own tongue, and she glanced at him from the corners of her eyes, astonished. Then she went away, but later she returned with a gourd and cool water from the spring.

Was it kindness or because they wanted him strong for dying?

In the woman he decided it was kindness, yet the others did not object, and they missed nothing. The woman was the squaw of one called Emiliano.

It was good to live. How could a man prepare himself for

death with the smell of the desert in his nostrils? What he wanted was not to die, but to live, to return again to Angie . . . and to Johnny.

He had always wanted a son. But what man does not want a son? What man wishes to die and leave no man to carry on, to continue the strain, the bloodline? Who wishes to waste what he has learned? Who wishes to see it die with him?

Old as life is the desire for sons. Old as all life upon the planet. It is this that carries on the species, and it is necessary for each man and woman to breed. That was the will of nature. All else came after. The species must continue, it must go on.

So there is deeply seated this desire, this wish. And he, Hondo Lane, what did he have to pass on? His skill with a gun? His ability to kill? To destroy?

No . . . but there were the desert and the mountains and the love of strong things, man things. The creak of saddle leather in the sun, the taste of cold, clear water, the ways of wild game and of horses, the little tricks of working . . . all these were ancient instincts, basic in the blood of man, built upon the ancient drive to carry on the race, the blood, the species.

And he sat here ready to die . . . for what? He left behind him nothing. A few people who would remember for a day or an hour. A man needed something on which to build. A man without a woman, without a home, and without a child was no man at all.

Johnny. If there had been no son of his own, he could at least have given Johnny what he had learned, the way of the desert and mountains, the thousand tiny things he had learned for himself, in bitterness and struggle, and the philosophy, too.

The things he had learned that were right and good, the things that living taught him—must these die?

He stared across the *rancheria* at the lonely squalor of the Apache camp, and knew that he must live. He must go on. He was not ready to die. He had done nothing, nothing at all.

And these people—how could he blame them? They were the People. That was what their name meant. They had believed they were meant to be the People. Yet when the first Americans came they had greeted them with friendship, and had been met with war. Then fiercely they had fought back. Not one but knew he fought in vain. They saw the white men endlessly coming, their many soldiers, their many ponies, their food supply that was endless, and their many cartridges of brass.

The Apache knew his hour was past. He knew the white men would take even his last land, but it was not in him to knuckle under. He would fight, sing his death song, and die. And he, Hondo Lane, was only a small part of the much vaster picture, and it mattered not at all to that picture that he was not through living, that he left things undone, that he wanted a son, that a woman waited for him. Or did she?

Yet there was no doubt even as his mind framed the question.

He had kissed her because a woman should not die unkissed, unloved. Yet after the kiss it had not been the same. He had gone away, yet even as he rode he knew he would return. And here he was, a prisoner beside the fire, awaiting the death by torture of the most fiendishly skillful of all savage torturers.

Vittoro got to his feet, and as upon a signal the others arose also, and then they moved toward him, and he sat quietly upon the ground and watched them come.

Here it was.

They grabbed him then and threw him back upon the sand and staked his arms out. Then with a piece of bark Silva scooped glowing coals from the fire and poured them into Hondo's open palm.

He felt the pain shoot through him, smelled the burning of his own flesh, but he stared at Silva and said bitterly, "Silva is a scalper of children, a runner after rabbits!"

"This only begins. We Apaches are patient." Silva looked his hatred and his triumph.

Beyond Vittoro a couple of braves had found Hondo's saddlebags and were going through them. Suddenly one straightened, grunting. He had found the tintype of Johnny, and he walked swiftly to Vittoro and thrust the picture before him.

Hondo saw the action, his teeth shut tight against the awful pain of his burning flesh.

Vittoro came suddenly to his feet and kicked the embers from Hondo's palm. "Loose him!"

A couple of Indians moved to obey, and Silva sprang between them and the prisoner, his face dark with angry blood. "It shall not be so!"

Vittoro's voice was even, cold. "I have need of this man."

"It shall not be!"

Vittoro glared at him, then snapped at the others, "Obey!"

As they slashed Hondo's bonds and released him, Silva shouted, "I claim the blood right!" He was beside himself with fury. "It is my privilege. It is so written."

Hondo looked down at his charred hand. Huge blisters were already beginning to shape, yet the hand was not so badly burned as he had believed, or so deeply. It was a hard hand, calloused by much work and much handling of guns. Now it was burned and crippled for a time, but a hand still, with fingers to move and to grip.

The medicine man had come forward with knives. Hondo was scarcely aware of what they did. He clutched the wrist of the burned hand and looked down at it, his face twisted with agony.

Then he heard, through his pain, the muttering words of the medicine man, blessing the knives, and he looked up suddenly.

"That life may ebb cleanly."

"That life may ebb cleanly," Vittoro repeated. "It is so written."

Silva stripped off his jacket, a lithe, powerful warrior in the prime of his young manhood. Vittoro stepped to a quickly drawn circle and flipped a knife into the ground on each side.

"White man, do you understand?"

"I lived with the Mimbreños many winters."

He came swiftly to his feet, only to stagger from the clumsiness of his recently released feet. Silva swooped for a knife, and Hondo caught his in his burned palm, then threw it, as one would a gun doing the border shift, to his left hand. He caught the knife deftly, and Silva sprang close, his eyes glowing with eagerness.

Hondo circled, knowing the danger of the man. He was strong, uninjured, and filled with hatred. Under any circumstances he would be dangerous. Silva extended his left hand, but was bothered by the knife in the wrong hand. It should have been in the right, so he could seize the wrist. Circling to study this, he lunged suddenly. Hondo felt the sharp point of the knife rip his shirt, then he stomped down hard with his boot on Silva's bare foot and slashed with his knife edge. The Indian twisted away but the knife left a red line that rapidly turned red with blood along a shoulder.

They circled, and around them the sweaty faces stared eagerly. Hondo could hear the breathing of the warriors. He could see the glow of firelight, he could see the eagerness in their eyes, for this to them was the great moment, the greatest of sport. Fighting men all, they could know and respect a fighting man, and not one there but knew the odds each man faced.

Silva came in low, his point flicking. Hondo sprang back, then lunged. The knife of Silva stabbed and the blade sank into Hondo's shoulder.

Before it could be withdrawn, Hondo pressed forward against the haft, holding the knife in the wound to prevent its withdrawal. They went to the ground and Hondo caught Silva's hair and forced his head back, exposing the brown throat, then he put the edge of his knife against the throat of the Indian and looked up at Vittoro.

Vittoro stood above them and he said, unhurried, "The white man permits you to choose, Silva."

Silva hesitated, his hatred a living, fighting thing. Yet there was only the one choice, to yield or to die. And he was not ready to die. If he lived he might yet kill the white man and take his hair.

"I choose," he muttered.

Vittoro gestured, and Hondo released Silva and stepped back. But he still held the knife.

Silva stared at Hondo, then turned abruptly and stalked away to his wickiup.

"White man," Vittoro said, "is it in your thoughts you have purchased life?"

"It is my thought that the one called Vittoro is a great chief, and a chief considers all that happens in this world."

"It is possible you may live. Or you may die. We shall see what is written."

FIFTEEN

A cross the vast sweep of the sky there were clouds, darkening clouds pressing ominously down toward the far hills. Flat upon the earth, skyward they lowered in huge, unbelievable masses.

A low wind caught the breath of their coolness and moved across the desert, moving down the arroyos and canyons, creeping across the face of a land scarred by canyons and ridged by the backbones of ancient ridges. And the cool wind came swiftly and crossed the land and dipped into the basin and the ranch.

The wind stirred the curtain and Angie looked up from her ironing and glanced outside. A few leaves skittered across the hard-baked clay of the yard, the horses' tails streamed past their hocks, and a whisp of hay blew to a corral post, then hung there, still and quiet.

Angie walked to the stove and exchanged her iron for one freshly heated, testing it with a dampened finger. At the window Johnny stared at the towering battlements of cloud, looming now above the basin's edge.

"Mommy, big clouds are coming up."

"It feels like rain." She drew the apron over the end of the board and sprinkled it lightly.

126

"Why is rain, Mommy?"

"God's way of making the earth green. This is what the Indians call the planting rain."

The planting rain. . . . She looked quickly past the trees at the sky.

Black, threatening clouds piled high. Quickly she put down the iron and went to the door, apprehension written large upon her face.

There could be no doubt. There would be rain, the planting rain, and then there was no time. When the storm began it would rain hard, then it might settle down for a long hard rain. They must leave before it ended, while it would still wipe out their tracks.

She folded her clothing and put it away, then went quickly to the cupboard. She packed swiftly, according to plan. She was sure, definite in her movements. There was no choice, no further decision to be made. Before the Indians could come, she must be gone.

Going to the bed, she took blankets and the old ground sheet and wrapped them in a tight roll. Johnny turned from the window. She caught his glance. "Would you like to go on a picnic, Johnny? In the rain?"

He looked doubtful. "In the rain?"

"It would be fun in the rain. We've got to ride a long way, and you'll have to take good care of Mommy."

"You mean I can ride a horse? All my own?"

"Yes, all your own. You can ride Old Gray."

Instantly he was all eagerness. She gave him several small tasks to do, then went to the barn and after some trouble lured the horses to the corral bars and got a rope on them. Leading them to the barn, she turned to the saddles. Hearing Johnny call out, she turned.

It was too late. A small cavalcade of Indians was coming down the slope.

Her heart pounding heavily, she walked to the house. "Johnny, you stay inside. They want to see Mommy."

There were a dozen Indians in the little group, and they had a prisoner. She saw that at once, only seeing the hanging head of a man, the dim shape of a haggard face beneath the hat. Vittoro dismounted and came to her. Behind him the man was dragged from the saddle.

"Is this your man?"

Angie looked beyond him. The man had lifted his head and he stared into her eyes. His own were glazed with suffering and weariness. She could see that something was terribly wrong with his hand. But she noticed nothing, only that it was Hondo Lane, and that he had come back.

"Speak!"

At a gesture from Vittoro, an Indian threw a pail of water into Lane's face. He blinked, then shook his head, straightening a little. Their eyes met and held.

"Is this your man?"

She understood suddenly, and she smiled quickly at Vittoro, coming down from the steps. "Yes. This is my husband."

She went to him quickly, taking his arm. Vittoro stared at her, then at Hondo Lane.

"White man," he said sternly, "you have lived with the Apache. That is good. You know how the Small Warrior should be taught so that he will be the honored son of Vittoro.

"Watch like the hawk, be patient as the beaver and courageous as the puma that he may learn well. Know it, then, or your dying will be long before you welcome death."

He turned away and mounted. Without looking back, the Indians rode from the valley.

Holding tight to his arm, for she sensed his weakness, she led him toward the house. In the distance thunder rumbled and there were scattered drops of rain, large drops striking hard on the baked clay.

She took him to the bed and he sat down, then fell loosely into sleep. She looked down at the blistered and swollen hand, the lacerated wrists, the bloody shirt. Turning quickly, she went outside with the pail to get fresh water.

Sam was coming down the slope, making slow time on three legs. She started to call, then saw Silva. The Apache came over the slope and started for the dog on a gallop. Sam turned, trying to run, but with a shrill yell Silva dropped his lance and ran the dog through the body. In a wild, despairing effort, the dog snapped at the lance, then fell free. Silva rode on over the slope.

Leaving the pail, Angie ran up the slope to the dying dog. His body was horribly torn; blood was flowing from him. Nothing could be done. She touched his head gently. "Good boy, Sam," she said softly. Feebly he tried to lick her hand.

She straightened then and looked in the direction Silva had taken. She knew then how a man could kill.

Rain was falling fast when she reached the house with her bucket. Once inside, she closed and barred the door. Quickly she got water on the fire to heat, got out the bandages she had made for emergencies. She had turned the horses back into the corral, and there was shelter for them under the overhang of the lean-to.

With a needle she ran a bit of colorless yarn previously soaked with antiseptic through each blister to allow it to drain. Then she put grease over the burned hand and wrapped it, not tightly. She was taking off his shirt when he sat up groggily.

"I'm all right."

"You will be when I fix your shoulder. The cut on your chest is only a scratch."

"It's not that. I've other things to keep me awake."

She looked at him quickly, thinking he had seen Silva's killing of Sam. "You saw it, then?"

"Saw what?"

"Silva. He finished Sam. Sam is dead. I'm sorry."

He held himself still, looking down at the clumsy-looking hand and its loose bandage. Sam . . . a man's dog.

"He was gettin' old. . . . Been with me goin' on eleven years. Old for a dog."

She was furious. "That beast Silva killed him. For no reason."

"Silva's scalp lock should be dryin' from a ridgepole."

"I know how you feel. That loyal dog, and . . . and . . ."

Hondo turned the bandage, looking at it. She could not see his expression, only hear his voice. He was keeping his eyes down.

"Wasn't he an ugly cuss, that Sam? Mean as a catamount in the breeding season. I almost ate him once. Up on the Powder. Quick freeze caught us, and after I'd been three days without rations, I took to looking at Sam.

"Lucky for him I found us a snowbound moose. Didn't look forward to eatin' Sam. Probably been tougher than a trail-shiny moccasin."

Angie turned down the light and moved away. She could sense the man's grief, and she was feeling it herself. That brutal, ugly-looking mongrel . . . and there at the last, dying, he tried to lick her hand.

A fighting dog, so strangely gentle. The thought moved her and she looked quickly at the man who lay face to the wall.

So strangely gentle. . . .

Did the dog take on the qualities of the man? Or under the hard exterior were they much the same?

She turned to her work and saw the rolled-up blankets she had meant to take away. Now she need not go.

But what had she done? Her face turned crimson. She had told Vittoro this man was her husband! And he dared not leave now.

Yet what else could she have done? Had she not accepted him as her husband, he would have been killed, and she would have no choice but to become a squaw to one of Vittoro's braves. Still, what must he think of her?

Outside thunder rumbled and rain was falling, falling steadily, without the fury of the storm that had come those long days ago after he had ridden away before. She added fuel to the fire. A gust of wind sent a little smoke into the room. Then a big drop fell down the chimney and hissed upon the coals.

Johnny had already gone to bed, sleeping contentedly. The man was back.

And outside the rain was no longer a threatening thing, but

suddenly it made the house seem even cozy, very warm. She listened to the heavy breathing of Hondo. Was this what she wanted? A man in the house?

No, not a man. *This* man . . . and no other.

He turned, muttering in his sleep, and something fell to the floor with a tinny sound. Glancing down, she saw it was a tintype. She picked it up. Johnny. But the tintype was scarred. Instinctively she knew what that scar meant.

Turning, she went to him and thrust it back into the pocket from which it had fallen.

For a long time she sat at the table, staring at the rain-streaked window. There was nothing to think of now, nothing to wait for. There was only the night and the steady rain falling, and the quiet, good sound of a man breathing heavily in his sleep. She knelt beside the fire, and banked it with a log, and then another, gathering the coals close.

When she got up, she brushed her hands down, straightening her apron. She looked over at his broad back, at muscles relaxed and sleeping now. She wanted to touch him, to put her hand upon his hair. . . .

She turned quickly to her own bed and began to undress. A large drop hissed on the dying coals, a stick popped loudly. There was rain on the roof, but it was quiet in the house, and there was no fear. The man was back.

SIXTEEN

When she awakened it was daylight and the house was silent. Suddenly, and with a start, she realized that Johnny was gone, and so was Hondo.

Glancing through the window, she could see Hondo at the corral, Johnny beside him. They were pitching hay to the horses. Quickly she dressed.

The ground was wet, and rain dripped from the eaves, but the rain had stopped for the moment. There was no break in the clouds. When she had breakfast started she returned to the mirror and fixed her hair more carefully.

When she opened the door, Hondo glanced around. "Breakfast is ready!" she called, and he started to the barn with the fork. Together they trudged toward the house, and after Johnny had bathed, Hondo followed.

His hair was freshly combed when he came in, but he was favoring his bandaged hand and his shoulder was stiff. He avoided her eyes, seating himself quickly. They ate in silence, and when his cup was empty she reached for the pot. "More coffee?"

"Thanks."

He was silent, brooding. Once he started to speak, then stopped.

132

"After breakfast you'd better take off your shirt and let me fix it."

He gulped his coffee, then said quickly, "Not before I show you something."

He took the tintype from his pocket and handed it to her. She looked at it, and then at him.

"Did Ed give it to you?"

"No. I took it off his body."

She had known this. She had felt it from the moment she saw the tintype with the bullet scar. Now she waited, but she felt nothing. There was nothing to feel. Later, she knew she would. But Ed . . . For months now he had seemed like somebody who had never really been. Like someone who had walked across the page of her life and left no tracks.

"He's dead."

When she had spoken the words, tears came to her eyes. There were no sobs, just a welling of tears. She sat silent, and no words came to help.

"I tried to tell you last night. I wanted to."

"I'm not surprised. It's . . . it's like something that happened long ago. I guess I never really expected him to come back."

Hondo tasted his coffee and tried to find the words to tell her the rest of it. But how did you tell a woman you had killed her husband? One of you had to be in the wrong. He was not prepared to accept the blame for trouble he had not wanted. Nor was he sorry for Ed Lowe. He was sorry only because the dead man had been the husband of Angie.

The door burst open and Johnny came charging back into the room. He rushed at Hondo, seizing his arm.

"Look out for his hand, Johnny." She crossed the room to the stove. "It's very noble of you."

"Noble?" Hondo looked at her under his brows. "Me?"

"You came in here to get us out."

"I'm going to give you something," Johnny said. "My Indian emblem. Vittoro gave it to me, didn't he, Mom?"

He started off quickly to get the headband. Hondo shifted

his feet under the table and allowed Angie to fill his cup again. He was deeply stirred. Johnny's prize possession, and he wanted him to have it.

Angie hesitated, putting the coffeepot back on the stove. "The Indians," she said at last, "place such a great value on dying well. Did Ed die well?"

"Yes, ma'am. Well."

Angie resumed the ironing halted by the coming of the Indians. Something in Hondo's attitude disturbed her, but she could not explain her feeling. It was unlike him to be so silent.

It was something about Ed. Something was wrong there, very wrong.

Nevertheless, she said, "When Johnny is old enough, and when he has to be told, it will make him proud."

Johnny came in with his emblem. He placed it on the table before Hondo. "Here's the emblem. You're a chief now!"

Hondo Lane turned away from the table and picked up the headband. He turned it in his hands, studying it. After a while he put it back on the table. Talking to a child . . . what did he know about that?

"Johnny," he said slowly, uncertain of what to say, "I'd like to take it, because that's a mighty fine gift. Guess there ain't anything you could give me that would be nicer. But you see, that headband was given to *you*, not to me.

"It was given to you by Vittoro. He meant it for you. Now I'd like to have you give me something, but this is yours: Wouldn't be right, nohow, to give it to me.

"Vittoro, he's a mighty big chief. Not many folks he likes. He must admire you quite some to give you that, so you stick by it.

"You an' me, Johnny, we got a lot of ground to cover together. Vittoro wants you to know how an Apache gets along. Good thing to know, too. You live in this country, you better know most of it. Man can never tell when he'll be lost in the desert, have to feed himself, find water, maybe. All that you've got to learn."

"Will you teach me?"

Hondo placed his hand clumsily on the boy's shoulder. "I reckon I'd like that, son. I sure would. I guess I've learned so much I'm up to here with it. Need somebody to learn it from me."

When Angie was washing clothes at the edge of a pool in the creek, Hondo rode down the slope with an antelope slung behind his saddle.

Angie looked up with a smile. "More fresh meat. We're living high."

Johnny sat on a round rock some distance above the pool, fishing.

Hondo swung down from the saddle and said quietly, "Don't turn around too fast, but there's an Indian up on the rim right now, just under that stunted pine."

"I can't see him. You must have wonderful eyesight."

"Learned. There was one up there day before yesterday, too."

He ground-hitched the lineback near a patch of grass, then walked back, starting to roll a smoke.

"Why? I don't understand."

"To watch the boy, I think. Vittoro must set store by him."

He left Angie to her washing and strolled upstream to where the boy was fishing. He took off his hat and ran his fingers through his hair. It was cool under the cottonwoods, better than out there on the desert. Was he getting soft? Or had this life got to him?

"If you want my opinion, you won't catch any fish there."

"He never does," Angie said, "but it keeps him amused."

"Might as well catch him a bass while he's at it." He glanced around, his brow furrowing. "Course, I don't mean to interfere."

"Please do."

She dipped a boy's shirt into the water, rinsing it. When she straightened up, she said quietly, "He needs a father. He's getting to that age now. He loves me, but I'm a woman. Sometimes he tolerates me."

Hondo grinned. "Boys are that way. Wait'll he gets older. He'll do mor'n tolerate a pretty woman."

She flushed a little, but she was pleased. "He has lots of time."

"Grow up before you know it."

"I . . . I don't want him to be here. Not when he's older."

"No, ma'am. But right now he's best off here. Boy should know how to hunt. How to get along. He'll learn better here, and you're safe, long as Vittoro lives."

She looked at him quickly. "You don't think I would be if he died?"

"Don't figure to scare you, but what'd you think about Silva?"

She remembered the hatred in the Indian's eyes, the way he started toward them that first day, the way he had killed Sam.

"He'll be the big man when Vittoro dies," Hondo said. "Do to think about."

Johnny trudged downstream to Hondo, who shoved his hat back on his head and looked down at the boy. "Where's the sun?"

"There." Johnny pointed.

"On the back of your neck." He indicated the shadow the boy threw upon the water. "Shadow. If you can see it, the fish can see it. Always fish with the sun in your face. That's if you want my opinion. And that bank's the place."

"Can I, Mommy?"

Angie hesitated. She was afraid of the creek. There were deep pools, and some old snags that had washed down from upstream. "Some of those pools are deep. I worry about him out here."

"He can't swim?"

"He's so young."

"I've seen Indian boys that age swim the Missouri at flood." He watched the boy lazily as Johnny started across the stream on the stones. At the far bank, Johnny stepped ashore. "Hey, boy!"

Johnny hesitated, looking back, and Hondo said, his voice carrying easily across the small stream, "Hot this time of day. Was I you, I'd walk on the sunny side of that rock. When it's hot the snake will be in the shade, when it's cold he'll be in the sun."

Johnny skirted the rock, then found a good place and seated himself, dropping his hook into the water.

"Funny thing. An Apache won't eat fish."

"What?" Angie was astonished. "I thought all Indians fished."

"What most folks think. Maybe it's because they live mostly in desert country, but no Apache will eat fish."

"I never heard of such a thing!"

"Fact. Down at Camp Grant the 'Pache kids used to hang around, beggin' candy or biscuits. When the pony soldiers got tired of havin' them around, they'd open a can of fish and set it out. They'd all leave." He threw the stub of his cigarette into the water. "Two reasons for that, though. Partly it was the fish, partly the label on the can."

"The label?"

"You know that red devil they have on some brands of fish? Scares Apaches. They call it ghost meat." Hondo squatted on his heels, watching her wash. "That Indian's gone from the rim."

"How do you know? You haven't looked up."

"I looked."

Angie dried her hands. "Do you think Vittoro really means it when he says he'll make an Apache out of Johnny?"

"If I were you I'd believe him. There's a lot of dead men that didn't believe what Vittoro said."

"He seems to love the baby."

"Baby? That kid's no baby. He must be five or maybe six."

"He's six. But he's still a baby."

"Time there was a man around here. Treat him like a baby and he'll be one. Spoils a boy to be protected. How'll he ever learn to care for himself?"

It was cool beside the stream. Hondo put his back against the trunk of a huge old cottonwood and watched the water. The clothes were drying in the sun, and Angie sat on a stone at the water's edge, her hair a little disarranged, lovely in the morning sun. Hondo Lane squinted his eyes at her, seeing her clear, poised beauty, yet uneasy at what lay between them.

The boy sat upstream, watching the line that hung into the

water, slow-moving at that point. Before Hondo it rippled over stones, chuckled into hollows, and slid silkily past the weathered trunk of a blown-down cottonwood, long dead.

He glanced at the lineback, lazily cropping grass in the shade, and then past him at the hills. A man could get used to this. He grinned when he thought of Major Sherry. He was probably throwing a fit by now, thinking him dead, his scalp hanging in some Apache wickiup.

"Mommy! Mommy! I caught one!"

Johnny came running across the rocks toward them with a fish flopping at the end of his hook. Hondo was unimpressed. He slashed a thong from his buckskin shirt. "You can gill him on this, if you want to."

"Thanks, Emberato."

Angie turned on Hondo. "He calls you Emberato all the time."

"My Apache name. I told him."

"What does it mean?"

Hondo shrugged, turning his shoulder against the tree. "You can't put Apache words into English. It means Bad Temper."

Angie looked at him again, studying the line of his profile. Bad Temper? How could he get such a name as that? Or had they taken him seriously with his growling? He was as gentle as his ugly brute of a dog had been. All Sam had needed was a chance. And a little petting. The thought made her flush, but it amused her, too, and she looked at him quickly. He was watching the boy with his fish.

Another thought occurred to her. "You cut that thong from your jacket. Aren't you afraid you'll have no ornamentation left if you cut off all that fringe?"

"Isn't for ornament. Not only. The fringe helps the buckskin to shed water. That's why it's there."

Johnny tied his fish to a stick and let it hang in the water, then he came back to Hondo and Angie.

"You say he can't swim?" Hondo sat up. "You do what you want to, but if it was me, I'd see the kid could swim." He reached out suddenly and picked Johnny up by the seat of the pants and threw him into the deepest part of the pool.

Angie sprang to her feet, crying out. She started to the pool and Hondo came to his feet quickly and put a hand on her shoulder.

Johnny surfaced, spluttering and floundering. Angie was furious. She struggled to pull away, but he held her, while Johnny, floundering but clumsily swimming, made his way to a rock. Clutching the rock, he turned to Hondo. "Emberato! I did it!"

"Just reach out your hand and grab a handful of water and pull it toward you, not too fast. Keep your fingers together so it won't get away. That's how I learned, if you want to know."

He released Angie, and she looked up at him, her anger dying. "Sometimes you're cruel."

"Am I? The kid can swim, can't he?"

He gathered the reins of his horse and picked the fish from the water. "I'll go clean the fish for him. Right he should eat it tonight, eat his own game himself."

"But how will he get back?"

"Swim."

"He may drown!" she protested, staring anxiously at Johnny, cheerfully kicking at the cool water.

"I don't think so."

He turned and walked off, leading the horse. Johnny yelled after him, then slid into the water and paddled awkwardly to the bank and climbed out. He was swelling with childish pride. "I swam, Mommy!" he said.

Hondo Lane had vanished toward the stable, and Angie took Johnny's hand and started toward the house. She was still not over her anger at his sudden and to her unbelievably brutal action. She mentally told herself he was cruel. He was rough. He was no fit man to be around a child. But the fact remained that now Johnny could swim.

SEVENTEEN

T he wind talked among the junipers and brushed cheeks
with the skeleton face of the cactus and along the hills
walked two horses and two riders. Hondo Lane, the killer from
the Brazos, and a boy of six, riding Old Gray.

They rode in silence through the morning, but Hondo's eyes
were careful on the desert. It was a gamble, taking the child
out this way, for there were other Apaches than those of
Vittoro, yet the boy must learn, and there was no better time
than now.

A bird flew up, sailed away a few yards, then vanished into
the brush. "See that bird? We'll ride his way. Want you to get
a good look at him."

The bird flew up again several minutes later. "It's a Gambel's
quail, Johnny. Drinks a lot, so you never find him too far from
water. Thing to remember."

They rode on. The sun was up and hot. They had brought no
lunch, deliberately.

As they rode on, Hondo pointed out plants used by the
Indians for food, for medicine, or for making fire. He had the
boy stop to examine the leaves, to learn how each one grew,
and whether on low ground or high mountain slopes. There

were other plants that the Indians gathered for making dyes or soap, or for their strong fibers.

"See the other fellow first," Hondo said. "Then you can let him see you or not, as you like. Never make a fire with smoke, even in good times."

He turned his horse wide around a boulder. "Best thing is a small fire, maybe under a tree. If there's any smoke at all, the branches and leaves will spread it out. There won't be no column.

"Use dry wood. Curl-leaf is good, never makes smoke. Look out for that rubber brush I showed you. Makes heavy, black smoke."

He drew up. "That there," he pointed at a broomlike shrub about four feet tall, "is *yerba del pasmo*. 'Paches chew the twigs for toothache."

They drew up a moment later at another plant. "Arrowweed. 'Paches make arrows from the straight stems. Use 'em for makin' cages an' baskets, too. Stuff smells good. Night, sometimes you can smell it quite a ways." They rode on, and after a bit he said, "Pimas use that arrowweed for makin' a tea for an eyewash."

On a hillside they saw some bones and part of an old hide. Hondo Lane drew up and rolled a smoke. "Deer," he said, nodding. "Dead a long time. See those tracks near it?"

"Yes." Johnny straightened in his saddle and peered at the tracks. "What are they?"

"Wolf. Bigger than a coyote."

"Maybe it was a dog."

"No. Dog walks right up to something. A wolf is suspicious. He circles around, stops, smells, smells the air. Wolf's more careful."

They rode alongside the dead animal. Only the bone and hide remained. "Cat now, cougar or *tigre*, you don't see claw tracks. Dog or wolf you do. Cat draws his claws back inside. Puma or cougar, no dif'rence in 'em, sometimes they don't leave tracks. Mighty light on their feet. If they got reason to, they can jump thirty feet."

They mounted a long slope, and Hondo talked on, forgetting time and distance, yet keeping his eyes always roving, always alert to point out something of interest. "Nobody but a fool or a tenderfoot wears bright, shiny stuff on his clothes. Only a fool would ride a white horse. See it too far off. That bright, shiny stuff is for sissies, townfolk. You wear it out here an' some Injun see you ten mile off by sun reflectin'. You'd lose your hair mighty quick."

Suddenly Johnny pointed. "There's one of those birds! The quail you showed me!"

"Sure is. You got a quick eye, son." He drew up. "Now it's gettin' nigh to noontime. Should be water not far off."

He studied the country carefully, and finally he turned the lineback down a long slope toward an upthrust of rock. "Could be down there. Water falls in rain an' sinks down. Sometimes underground water forms a sort of a pool above clay and along a layer of sandstone. If that's busted, there's liable to be a spring. Up ahead there, that ground is faulted. May be water there."

"I'm hungry," Johnny said suddenly.

"Me too." Hondo glanced at the boy. "Noticed any insects lately?"

"Bees. There was a bee on a flower back there. One flew off, too."

"Which way'd he go?"

Johnny scowled. Finally he pointed. "Thataway, I think."

"That's right. But don't have to think. You notice hereafter. Bees can take you to water. Need water, an' they go often. So you watch where they go."

He stopped his horse suddenly. Johnny drew up, looking at him curiously. Then, aware that something was expected of him, he looked around carefully. Suddenly he saw the rounded, ugly body of a golden and brown lizard lying near a rock. It was fat-tailed and repulsive. The boy instinctively drew his horse away from it.

"Gila monster, son. Mighty poisonous. You leave him alone, he'll leave you alone. No wild animal wants no truck with a

man. Up to you to keep away from him, or give him a chance
to get away from you. That there lizard, now, you watch out for
him. Mostly he don't aim to move. He likes it where he is."

A broken ledge of rock tilted sharply against the sky, a ledge
broken off in some bygone upheaval of the earth and thrust up
like a broken bone, splintered and ragged on edge. The wind,
blown sand, and rain had tapered those edges but little, yet on
the underside they found a hollow of water, a few desert
willows, and one cottonwood, still young.

Hondo swung down and helped the boy to the ground, then
led the horses into the shade to cool off. With Johnny helping,
he gathered dry sticks for a fire. A bee buzzed near them, then
another.

Hondo caught Johnny's arm and pointed. A small swarm of
bees hovered around a crack in the rock above them. "Hive up
there. Lots of honey, too."

"Can we get some?" Johnny was eager. "Can we get some
away from them?"

Hondo studied the situation. "Hard to get it, but maybe
later."

Earlier he had killed a rabbit, skinned and cleaned it, then
sprinkled it with salt. Now he broiled the rabbit over the fire,
then led the horses to water. He walked out away from the
rocks, keeping among the brush, and studied the terrain. Twice
that morning he had seen unshod hoofprints. There were Apaches
around.

He walked back to the boy and ate his share of the rabbit
while Johnny was brushing the spines from a tuna the way he
had shown him earlier. As the boy ate the desert fruit, he
thought about how fast the morning had gone, how much he
had enjoyed it. And this was the son of the man he had killed.

How could a man have left a boy like this alone? To say
nothing of Angie. What possessed a man with everything in the
world to live for to go to a post and spend his time gambling
and cheating passing strangers and soldiers from the post?

"We'll start back," he said suddenly. "Your mother may get
worried."

He thought of those unshod ponies. This boy had learned enough for one morning. There was no sense in taking a chance. While Johnny filled his canteen again, he walked back among the rocks to look in the opposite direction. Then he squatted suddenly.

Four Indians had come out of the wash along which they had ridden earlier. Even at this distance he could tell they were mountain Apaches, strange to this area. They were studying the ground, apparently puzzled.

If they had followed him far they would have occasion to be curious, for the horses had wandered from one point of interest to another, studying plants, tracks, and rocks. Now they were looking toward the serrated rock where lay the spring.

Hondo Lane turned and walked swiftly back. There was a hollow among the rocks. "Johnny," he said in a quiet voice, "we're in trouble. Mountain Apaches . . . not from Vittoro."

The boy, he thought suddenly, looked eager rather than frightened. He chuckled a little, and Johnny looked up at him and smiled. "Will we fight?" he said quickly.

"Not if we can help it," Hondo said. "An' don't be so durned eager, youngster. People get hurt fightin'."

He led the horses into the hollow of rock and they waited. Suddenly he heard a hoof strike rock, then he saw the slim brown bodies of the Indians. White Mountain Apaches, by their look. They were studying the tracks at the spring.

Hondo slid the thong from the butt of his six-shooter. "Trouble starts," he said, and his voice was flat and harsh, "get behind the rocks and stay there, you hear me?"

He stood up slowly, and almost at once the Apaches saw him. His rifle was in his hand. The distance was no more than forty yards.

"Hola, brothers!" He spoke clearly. He was aware that Johnny, unable to restrain his curiosity, had appeared beside him.

The Apaches stared, uncertain what to make of the strange pair. Yet soon he was puzzled himself, for they kept staring, and then they walked forward hesitantly. It was not Hondo himself at whom they stared, but at Johnny. Suddenly Hondo realized the boy was wearing Vittoro's headband. The opal had caught the light and reflected into their eyes. A white boy with an Apache headband puzzled them.

"The boy is Apache?"

The Indian sounded doubtful, for despite Johnny's deep tan, he was obviously a white boy.

"Blood brother to Vittoro!" Hondo made the name ring against the crags. "He is Small Warrior!"

Hesitantly, still wary of a trap, the Indians came forward. One of them hung back. His face was narrow and mean, with a cross-grained look about it. Hondo looked at this one, then never let the corners of his eyes stray away from him.

The Apaches stopped a dozen yards off, staring from the boy to Hondo. Rifles were hard to come by, and Hondo's was a new Winchester '73, firing seventeen shots without reloading. He wore a pistol also, and there were horses. Yet the name of Vittoro carried a large sound to Apache ears.

"What do you here?"

"The boy learns the way of the desert."

They accepted this and considered it. The wandering tracks were now explained. "It is the wish of Vittoro," he added. "Small Warrior is to be as an Apache on the desert."

Three of the braves were obviously interested, and as Johnny stood there beside Hondo Lane, he carried a certain indomitable look that amused and interested them.

"The Small Warrior takes scalps?" the nearest Apache asked, grinning.

Only the tall Indian who hung back disturbed Hondo. The others were fascinated by the stalwart youngster. The carriage and manner of Johnny was Apache, and it made them chuckle.

"The Small Warrior takes scalps?" the Indian repeated.

"Not of dogs or women!" Johnny had not listened to Vittoro for nothing. "Go in peace!"

One of the Indians shouted with laughter, and the three started to turn away.

The fourth Indian stood his ground, looking at Hondo. "This

one I know," he said suddenly. "He was scout for the pony soldiers."

There was sudden tension, and the other three turned quickly, looking from Hondo to their companion.

"I *was* scout for the pony soldiers," Hondo agreed. "I have lived among the Mimbreños also. This you do not like?"

There was challenge in his tone. It did no good to draw back or show hesitation.

"I have killed pony soldiers," the brave boasted.

"And I have killed Apaches."

They stared at each other. One of the others said something about Vittoro, but the tall Indian merely sneered. It was partly the rifle, partly the horses, but mostly it was that the Indian was a trouble-hunter. Hondo knew white men like him.

"I wear the scalp of a pony soldier on the mane of my horse!"

"An old pony soldier," Hondo said with contempt, "with white in his hair and age in his back."

"You are friend of Vittoro?" the Apache sneered. "I say you lie!"

Hondo ignored him. He spoke to the others. "The Small Warrior is the brother of Vittoro. Harm to him would mean blood feud. He is protected by Vittoro. I protect myself!"

He turned suddenly and struck the tall Indian across the mouth. It was a wicked, powerful blow, and the Indian staggered and fell in a heap.

An instant he lay there, eyes blazing, blood trickling from a smashed lip. Then like a cat he sprang to his feet and the rifle muzzle started to swing up. It was exactly what Hondo had wanted him to do. Deliberately he let the muzzle lift. Then he palmed his Colt and fired.

His rifle had been held by the barrel with his left hand. His right hand was free to grasp its trigger guard as it lifted if he elected to use it. The Colt came as a complete surprise.

The bullet struck the tall Indian over the heart and he grunted. His rifle's bullet dug earth at Hondo's feet, and then he fell face downward upon the ground.

To the unsuspecting Indians, who had never seen a fighter in action, the appearance of the Colt smacked of sheer magic. They stared at him, stared at the gun, and then they turned the Indian over and looked at the wound. Awed, they stared at Hondo.

Suddenly there was a clatter of hoofs and a dozen horsemen raced into the basin near the spring and ringed the small group. First among them was Vittoro. His hard old eyes looked first at Johnny, who stood close beside Hondo, his face white and still, but without tears or fear.

Then he looked at the other Indians, and Hondo spoke quickly. "Only one among them looked for war," he said. "That one is dead. These others are true men."

Vittoro stared at them and one Apache stepped forward. He held himself proudly. "We spoke in admiration of Small Warrior," he said. "This one wanted the scalp of that one." He pointed at Hondo.

Vittoro looked at them, then at Johnny. The Apache who had spoken then repeated what Johnny had said about not taking scalps of dogs and women, and Vittoro's hard old eyes glinted and the others chuckled. Nobody seemed much upset by the death of the tall Indian. Hondo holstered his gun. One of the others said something of that to Vittoro, speaking of the gun of magic. Vittoro looked at Hondo, then nodded. "The watcher of my brother is well chosen," he said. Then he lifted his coup stick and pointed at Johnny.

"Take the stick!" he commanded. "Count coup!"

Johnny hesitated. Hondo was suddenly glad that Angie was not present. "Johnny," he said distinctly, "you must do as Vittoro says. Take the stick he offers you and tap the Indian with it."

The boy's eyes were round and frightened. Yet he walked forward, his steps like those of an automaton, and, taking the stick, he tapped the dead Indian. Then he returned the stick and walked back to Hondo. His face was stiff and white but not a tear showed.

"Good!" Vittoro grunted. "Small Warrior soon be Big Warrior!"

Hondo took the boy and put him into his saddle, then he

stepped into the leather. He glanced over at the chief. "It has been a long day. Small Warrior has learned the tracks of the wolf and the *tigre*. He has learned the *yerba del pasmo* and the mescal, and many other things besides. He has caught game and cooked it, and he has counted coup. It is enough."

Vittoro nodded, and the two rode from the hollow of the spring, and scarcely were they on the desert when Johnny's face began to twist. With sudden instinct Hondo lifted him from the saddle, and then Johnny was crying. Startled to find himself holding a crying child, Hondo merely held him and said nothing.

After a long time, Johnny looked up at Hondo, but Hondo appeared not to notice. Then he leaned back against Hondo's arm and watched the desert.

Not until they were almost home did he get back into his own saddle.

"It was a hard thing," Hondo said. "You did well, Johnny."

"Look!" Johnny pointed. "There's some arrowweed!"

EIGHTEEN

The shock of seeing a man killed and being forced to count coup upon his body was a severe test for Johnny, yet Hondo noticed that he bounced back the next morning. He was a little more quiet, ready to remain at home for a day, but apparently no worse off for his experience. Hondo hesitated, then decided to tell Angie nothing about it for the time being. But she guessed something had happened, and finally he told her.

"Without the headband of Vittoro," Hondo told her, "we might have had a bad time of it."

"Or if you had not killed that man."

That silenced him. The killing of another man was very much in his thoughts. It seemed somehow wrong to have killed a woman's husband and to be here with her, not to have explained. Yet no matter how many times he tried to tell her, the words of explanation would not come. She sensed he was worried about something, and it bothered her.

He had returned to the house to replace his coffee cup and left her sitting beside the stream. Johnny was asleep. The tintype was on a shelf above his head. Hondo Lane stood and studied it, gnawing at his lip and thinking.

There was nothing else he could have done. It was a treach-

149

erous thing Lowe had attempted, and the man had been no good, not any way you looked at him. Still, he had to explain. He had to tell Angie, and he would tell her now.

It was late evening, not yet dark. The cottonwoods were at their endless whispering and the stream seemed unusually noisy tonight. Not loud, but with no other sound it was more obvious.

All day he had worked around the ranch, finding the little things to do that a handy man with tools can find on any such place. He had worked, always conscious of the woman up there at the house. This was as it should be . . . a man and a woman working toward something, for something. Not apart, but a team.

Leaving the house now, he walked across the yard toward where she sat alone by the stream. She turned to look up at him. In repose her face had a quality of true beauty that disturbed him. He knew she liked him, probably more. . . . But why should she? To him she was a woman, but a rare and wonderful thing, too.

"Angie, I've got something to tell you, and it's not gonna be easy."

"Then don't tell me yet." She lifted her face to the moon. The cottonwood leaves were like tiny silver mirrors, catching the light. "Just look. How odd the moon looks in this quarter! When I was a child my mother used to tell me it was a teeter-totter. You know, the tilted plank a child plays on. Do the Apaches have a name for it?"

"Bermaga, the planting moon . . . like they call the first rain the planting rain. Won't plant their corn until the moon's like that."

"You liked living with the Apaches, didn't you?"

He did not reply. The stream rustled against the banks, chuckled around the rocks as water does, and shimmered in the moonlight farther down. A horse stomped and blew in the corral.

"Don't have locks."

"I don't believe I understand."

"White man locks his cabin. No way to lock a wickiup. But you can be gone a whole season and your gear will still be there. Nobody steals. The old women with no men to provide for them . . . the chiefs drop half their kill at the old women's lodge before they take the rest home to feed their women and kids. Nothing selfish about an Apache. Yeah, I liked living with them."

She liked listening to his voice. It was slow, somehow restful, and underlying his words there was understanding, compassion. There was none of this you-get-along-on-your-own-or-die feeling. She had seen too much of that. The more people had, the more they felt that way. But this man had known loneliness and hardship.

"I think I would like that part of it, too. The way you speak of it."

"I know you would."

She tried to see his face in the deepening shadows, but outlines were gone, and she could only see where he was, not details or expression.

"Why did you decide that?"

Hondo shifted his boots, searching for the right words. "Because you're a warm woman. Because you can sit and watch a little boy doing something like drawing in the mud at the creek bank and the corners of your mouth wrinkle up and a man can see that what you're looking at makes you happy. Your hands are nice and clean when you put cooked meat down in front of a man, and your face is happy while he eats it."

Angie was surprised. She had not realized he had noticed these things. She felt a sudden desire to reach out in the darkness and touch him. Instead she said, "You notice everything. And thank you. Thank you very much."

A faint, far-off sound caught at his attention. He listened. There was nothing more.

She was close to him now. It was dark. He listened a moment longer.

"Angie, I've got to tell you somethin'. I'm not much for

lyin'—or for livin' a lie. Last time I was here, before Vittoro brought me . . ."

"Yes?"

"Rode some dispatch after that. Then there was some trouble. Killed a man." The sound came again then, closer. He reached out swiftly and drew her off the rock. His gun was in his hand. "There's someone in the willows."

"Do not shoot, white man." It was Vittoro's voice. He stepped from the trees. "Small Warrior has a knife. He sleeps with it."

"You were in the house?" Angie asked.

"Yes."

"Tell your brave behind us," Hondo said, "not to walk in the water. I like to killed him a few minutes ago."

Vittoro chuckled, then he said loudly, "Koori, you are very clumsy. Go to the horses."

"I almost threw a shot at him."

"He is very young. He will learn."

"If he lives."

"You are Apache." Vittoro paused a minute after the compliment, then turned to speak to Angie.

"A wickiup is an empty place without sons. Mine is an empty wickiup. I treasure Small Warrior. Now hear me! The pony soldiers are near. Soon will be fought a remembered fight. They will come here first. You will not go with them, white man."

"I will not go with them."

"The leader of the pony soldiers will question you. You will say you have seen the Apaches trailing to the west."

"This I will not do."

"You will not?"

"I will not."

There was a long moment of silence while the leaves rustled. Somewhere a fish jumped.

"You have a good man," Vittoro said at last to Angie. "Treasure him."

"I do!"

Vittoro was gone in the darkness. They stared after him,

eyes straining in the darkness, and then her arms were around him, her head against his chest.

An arm around her shoulders, he listened. "They're mounting up now."

"I don't hear a thing."

"Going off now. About eight, I'd say. Maybe nine."

She could hear nothing. The night was silent to her . . . and then she did hear something.

"There's something in those trees."

"Squirrel. Talking woke him and he's put out. There are nine Indians."

She drew back from him, looking up. His face was vaguely visible now, for the stars were bright and the moon was low over the trees.

"I love you."

She said the words suddenly, surprising even herself. Her hand went to her mouth. "I didn't mean to say that . . . but I did mean it. I *did*. I know it's an unseemly thing—my husband so shortly dead and . . ."

"I don't guess people's hearts got anything to do with calendars."

He kissed her gently, holding her close, and for a moment they were silent.

"You were wonderful, refusing to lie for Vittoro."

"Figure he was testing me. Indians hate a lie. I got to feel the same way. But I guess there's sometimes when a man has got to lie, if it makes it easier for someone."

"I feel strange . . . new. Well, like music. I am being silly, aren't I?"

"No. The Apaches have a word . . . Like I said, I can't explain it. As close as I can come is 'happy breathing.' "

"Kiss me again."

Their lips met in the darkness, clung, and then she leaned against him and for a long time they did not talk. It was growing cooler. The moon was down now, below the line of hills. Somewhere a coyote sent his lonely cry at the wide sky. An owl called.

"Don't think I'm crazy, but tonight I just couldn't bear to sleep under a roof with the moon and all. I'll go get some blankets."

"I'll get them if you want."

"No, I want to. A squaw would. I want to feel like a squaw woman. Feels good. Real good."

She moved away into the darkness and he listened to the water over the stones. Behind him the squirrel chattered.

Hondo sat up and looked around. "Squirrel, if you bother me some more, I'll eat you in a stew tomorrow."

The squirrel chattered inquiringly, and then there was silence. The water rustled, and at the house a door closed and then there were footfalls. Hondo Lane got up, moving back nearer the trees. "Better here," he said when she was close. "Leaves under the trees. Anybody comes, we'll see them first."

She handed him the blankets and the ground sheet and he shook them out, then put them down under the trees. Angie got down on her knees and spread the ground sheets over the leaves, then the blankets.

"You never forget, do you? I mean about seeing things first."

"Hope I never."

He was oddly uncomfortable, hesitant. "Good way to lose your hair, not noticing things."

He sat down and pulled off his boots. The cottonwoods whispered more softly. The squirrel gave one short, inquiring chatter, then was silent.

The lone coyote spoke to the sky and the stream rustled busily about the stones. A bit of mud fell into the stream with a faint plop.

It was night, and there was no sound. Or anyway, not very much.

NINETEEN

H ondo Lane turned from tightening the wheels of Angie Lowe's wagon to watch the column of cavalry file into the basin and past the butte. It was a sight to behold. Glittering, yes, but more than that, for these were part of the force that Lord Wolseley, then commander in chief of the British army, had declared was the finest fighting force in the world—and they looked it.

And, Hondo reflected as he stood beside Angie and Johnny, they had better be!

When the men were dismounted outside the ranch yard, the officer in command and the scout rode over to Hondo and Angie. The lieutenant dismounted, and behind him Buffalo swung down.

The lieutenant was impeccably garbed. His uniform was perfect in tailoring and perfect in military requirements. He walked to a position in front of Hondo and stopped, shifting his gloves. Heels together, he bowed.

"Madam and sir, may I present myself? Lieutenant McKay, Squadron D, Sixth Cavalry."

Behind him, Buffalo grinned at Lane. "Hi, Hondo, you old cabin-robber! Lieutenant, this is Hondo Lane. He's scouted some and rode dispatch for the cavalry. I don't know this here lady."

"Mrs. Lowe . . . Lieutenant." Hondo grinned at Baker. "Hi, Buff."

"You people are lucky," Lieutenant McKay assured them. "Obviously Vittoro and his renegades just happened not to find this hidden valley."

"Vittoro's been here," Hondo said. "Lots."

"And you live? One lone man stood off Vittoro?"

"No lone man stands off Vittoro. Not for long, anyway. He lets us live here."

"He's our friend," Angie said.

"Friend? Vittoro?" Lieutenant McKay was astonished. "Ma'am, I dislike saying such a gruesome thing in a lady's presence, but there are almost a thousand dead settlers on both sides of the border, scalped by this cowardly criminal."

Hondo lifted an eyebrow. "Vittoro may be a criminal by the book. I don't know. But if he's a coward it never showed up yet."

"Amen!" Buffalo said.

"My men will bivouac here for the night," McKay said, then he turned. "I must disagree with you, Mr. Lane. He has run before us for two hundred miles. My scouts and outriders report his band before us every day, yet each time we start to come to grips to fight an engagement, he runs."

"Indians got a story," Hondo said, "about a hunter who chased a puma until he caught him. Then it was the other way around."

McKay smiled. "That story goes back further than the Indians know. It is originally attributed to the first Roman army to enter Tartary. The soldier caught a Tartar and yelled out. His officer called back to come in and bring his prisoner, and the soldier replied, 'The Tartar won't let me.' "

McKay chuckled at his story, but neither Hondo nor Buffalo was amused.

"It's one of the favorite stories of Colonel Mays, who teaches cavalry tactics at the Point. The story is world-wide."

Hondo rolled a smoke. "How long you been out of West Point, Lieutenant?"

McKay hesitated, not liking to answer. He was afraid he knew what the question implied, and he did not like to appear a greenhorn. "Graduated class of '69, sir." His ears grew a little red. It was not long ago, and he resented the doubt of his ability the question seemed to imply, yet he was no fool. He had heard Major Sherry and even General Crook speak of Hondo Lane with respect.

"That story you told," Hondo said, "can be almighty true right here. You hear about Fetterman?"

"Lieutenant Colonel Fetterman, sir? You mean the massacre?"

"Well," Hondo said, "call it what you like. Fetterman was a good man, I guess, but he made the mistake of takin' the Sioux too lightly. He said give him eighty men an' he'd ride through the whole Sioux Nation. Remember what happened?" Hondo touched his tongue to his cigarette. "He had eighty-three men, an' he lasted less than twenty minutes."

McKay flushed a little. "I know. Ambush, wasn't it?"

"In a way. Ambush they led him into because he was big-headed." Hondo smiled. "You ain't that sort, Lieutenant, but don't take Vittoro lightly. Napoleon never knew anything that old 'Pache don't know."

"Oh, come now, sir!" McKay was astonished, half believing he was being led on. "You don't mean that!"

"I do mean it." Hondo was dead serious. "Lieutenant, what would you say was the main object of a leader facing a superior force?"

McKay's eyes searched Hondo's. He was curious, and suddenly aware there was more to the man to whom he talked than a knowledge of the desert and Indians.

"Why . . . why, offhand, sir, I'd say to harass the enemy, to fight a delaying action until he could get him on ground of his own choosing, but at all costs to preserve his own force intact."

Hondo nodded. "I'm no military man, Lieutenant, but I'd say you couldn't go far wrong on that plan. And ain't that what Vittoro's been doing?"

Lieutenant McKay's brow puckered. "Well . . . yes," he admitted, "after a fashion."

Buffalo grinned at Hondo after the Lieutenant had moved off to inspect the bivouac area. "Gave him somethin' to puzzle over, you did." He chuckled. "Got a sight to learn, that one." Then he nodded. "But he's all right, I think. I like him. Only I wish it was the Major out here in command."

Lieutenant McKay turned toward the house, where Angie had stopped at the door. "Mrs. Lowe, my orders are to make a clean sweep as far as Twin Buttes. We will go on to Twin Buttes tomorrow and return tomorrow night to escort you and your boy out to safety."

"We're safe. We have Vittoro's word."

"The word of an Indian criminal!" McKay was incredulous. "Even if Lane is willing to take the risk, I don't think you should."

"I'll take his word. We'd rather stay."

"I'm sorry. My orders are to bring out any settlers who have survived." He hesitated. She was such a pretty woman, and he did not like to think of leaving her here. He had been on the frontier only a few weeks, but he had already seen the bodies of some of the settlers. It had not been a pretty sight. "I . . . if you will excuse me, ma'am."

Hondo and Buffalo had come to the house. "He's very nice," Angie said, "and very young."

"Yes, ma'am," Buffalo agreed, a shadow of worry in his tone, "he sure is."

"You been scouting for this patrol?"

"This is about the twentieth day I had them out, Hondo. Many a scalp's been took."

Angie looked down at Johnny. "You watch Lieutenant McKay, Johnny. That's the kind of manners I want you to have." She turned back to the men. "And he has such handsome eyes. And that beautiful black, curly hair."

"That hair will be hanging from the top pole of an Apache wickiup." He looked over at Buffalo. "This little-boy lieutenant will get you killed."

Buffalo shrugged. McKay was not the first he had seen come to Indian country. Nor, with luck, would he be the last. Some of them had it, some of them did not. Some were only pretty, some were all spit and polish, and some of them sharpened down into first-class fighting men. There had been Major Powell, for instance, up at Kearney. Had he taken the command the day Fetterman went out . . . It was useless to think of that. Fetterman had outranked him, forced the issue, and gone glory-hunting with eighty-odd better men.

"You know how it is," Buffalo said. "Us scouts got to get these young officers educated."

Suddenly he remembered. "Say, you rec'lect how you whupped me at the post? My medicine must have been bad. You busted off a tooth and it went to hurting so bad I had to go to the barber so he could pull out the rest of the tooth. Partner, that *hurt*! Did I catch you that day, I'd have set your sun for you. You'd never have seed another morning."

Angie came to the door, drying her hands. "Hondo, I notice the soldiers are starting their food fires. I naturally can't invite very many to eat with us in the cabin, but if your friend Mr.—uh . . ."

"Yeah, Buffalo will eat with us." He turned to look at the big buffalo hunter. "We've known each other eight or ten years. You got to have a last name. Or have you?"

Buffalo looked up sharply, offended. "Sure I got a last name. What do you think I am?" He tried to emulate the Lieutenant's bow. "Mrs. Lowe, my name is . . ." He hesitated, and his face got red. "Baker. That's what it is, Baker." He sneered at Hondo. "Didn't think I had any last name!"

Buffalo looked around slowly. "Been tryin' to figure what this place reminds me of, Hondo. It's that ranch of your'n in California. Where we stayed before we went to fight with those people up north. Under a bluff just like this, creek and mesa spreading out . . ."

Angie looked up at Hondo. "You have a place that looks like this?"

"East of San Dimas.

"Just like this. Reminds me all to . . ." He hesitated, took a quick look at Angie, and ended weakly, "Reminds me. It sure does."

"You can wash in the basin on the bench. Towel hangin' right there."

"Wash? Towel? Oh, sure."

"It's wonderful, Hondo. About your place, I mean. That our tastes are so similar. You picked a basin with a creek, as I did."

"I guess we could winter in the same lodge without nobody getting their throat cut in the night."

They stopped at the door, watching the camp settling down. There was an Indian up on the bluff again, but that was to be expected and Hondo said nothing until Buffalo walked up, drying his hands. Buffalo mentioned it, and he nodded. "Seen him. No use mentionin' it to the Lieutenant. He'd send out a patrol to catch him, an' these boys need their sleep."

Buffalo hung the towel on a peg near the door. "Don't you peg the Lieutenant too low. He's young, but he's different than some. He'll listen, an' he ain't afraid to ask questions. Most of 'em figure they got to know it all."

Buffalo looked awkwardly at the table. Angie had taken out her red-checkered cloth and there were napkins of the same color by the plates. Buffalo looked around, embarrassed. "I ain't et—ate—at a table like this in a coon's age, ma'am. Reckon I'm some rusty."

She smiled. "We're hoping you'll eat with us often, Buffalo, so don't be afraid."

Buffalo blushed, then as the significance of her remark reached him he looked quickly at Hondo and started to speak, but Hondo scowled at him and he closed his mouth.

When they had finished, Angie got up and took down an apple pie and started to cut it, then she turned. "Hondo, would you like to ask the Lieutenant to join us for pie and coffee? I'm sure he'd like it."

When Hondo was gone, Angie turned quickly and looked at Buffalo. "Mr. Baker," she said quietly, "I want to ask you a question. Did you know Ed Lowe? My husband?"

"That no-a—" As the significance of her last words reached him, he broke off sharply. "Yes," he said after a minute, "I knew him."

She hesitated, then turned back to her pie. That explosive beginning answered her question in part, at least. Buffalo Baker said no more, and when the Lieutenant came in, she was talking about the Indians.

Buffalo excused himself and the Lieutenant sat down. He glanced quickly at Johnny, then smiled.

Lieutenant McKay might know little of Indian fighting, but he understood the things a lonely woman wants to know. He talked briefly of things at the post, then of what women were wearing in Washington, New York, and Richmond. After several minutes he switched the subject. He glanced sharply at Hondo. "What do you think Vittoro will do now? Will he keep running?"

"No. Not far, anyway. He's ready to fight."

"Mr. Lane, my business is to command, but I've been thinking of what you said. I'm not above taking advice. You know the Apaches. What would you advise?"

Hondo looked at his coffee. There was no doubting the earnestness of this man, and he had a sudden hope that whatever happened, this man might live. They needed men on the frontier who could learn.

"Can't advise you, Lieutenant. Only when you come up to him, it'll be because he's ready. If he's ready it'll be because he figures he can beat you or hurt you mighty bad. So when you come up on him, look around, because whatever you don't expect, that's what he'll do."

TWENTY

When Buffalo had finished sharpening his knife, Hondo
moved to the grindstone. Lennie Sproul lounged near the
barn, and Hondo felt irritation strong within him. Lennie Sproul
had been on the frontier for fifteen years, a lean, saturnine man
with a cynical eye and a way of showing up with unexpected
money.

Hondo Lane possessed no quality of the hypocrite. He was a
man whose likes and dislikes were obvious. His distaste for
Sproul was especially obvious.

The scout lounged nearer in his greasy buckskins and stood
watching the knife edge on the grindstone.

"Mighty fine rifle in your saddle scabbard. Always envied
you that there gun. Hard to come by, that new issue."

"Keep your hands off it." Hondo was short.

Lennie Sproul watched the grindstone for several minutes
while Hondo Lane's anger mounted. Sproul was not here by
accident. There was something on his mind.

"Knowed you ten years," Sproul said. "Never worked a day
beside you."

"Don't like you," Hondo replied, testing the edge of the
blade.

"Figured you didn't. But now I think you might admire to give me that there rifle."

Too astonished for reply, Hondo looked up, staring at Lennie, who answered with a broken-toothed smile. "Ways out of the post I come across some bodies. One of 'em was this lady's husband. Horse tracks around there, an' one set belonged to your lineback."

Hondo waited, his heart pounding heavily, anger building hard within him. Not the irritation he had felt for a disliked and disagreeable man, but the hard anger of a man.

"Nice setup you got here. Nice ranch, pretty woman."

Hondo took a slow, deep breath. He knew himself and he wanted no violence. Not the kind to which he was impelled.

"You can get yourself killed acting like this." He said the words slowly, taking his time, hoping the words would be a warning, that Lennie Sproul would know when to stop.

There was no stopping in the mind of Lennie Sproul. He had felt Hondo Lane's dislike keenly, but there had been nothing he could do. Now he saw the gun fighter's strength and skill humbled, his proud, easy manner broken. Why, the man had a ranch here. There was no telling what all he might get from him, given time.

Knowing triumph, he felt no discretion. "Could be I could get killed," he said with a smirk, "or I can get that new-fashioned Winchester. You didn't bushwhack that lady's husband, but it could look mighty like it. Did she know what happened, I don't reckon you'd set so well around here."

Hondo Lane dropped the knife and came up in one smooth, perfectly timed flow of motion. Lennie, too late, tried to step back. Hondo Lane's right fist caught the angle of his jaw and knocked him thirty feet into a heap on the ground.

The last staggering steps had carried Sproul past the lean-to stable and he had fallen in view of the cow corral.

Hondo Lane rushed after Lennie, who started to get up. He scarcely reached his feet before Lane struck him. Two hard punches, left and right. He hit the ground hard and Lane lifted a moccasined heel to stomp him when he saw Angie.

She was just rising from the stool beside her cow, the milk pail in one hand, the stool in the other. Nothing was needed beyond her expression. She had heard it all.

For a long moment their eyes held, searching, measuring, then she turned to walk away.

Lennie seizing his chance, crawled a few feet, then got to his feet and hurried away, a hand to his jaw.

At that instant Lieutenant McKay walked up to them. He looked at Lane. "We are about to leave, Mr. Lane." He faced Angie. "Mrs. Lowe, I hope you will not mind if Hondo accompanies us for half a day. We'd like him to go with us as far as Single Butte. It's rough country, I heard, and none of the other scouts knows that country. He can be back by tonight, so you will not be alone long."

"No, of course not."

McKay bowed, then turned to Hondo. "If you will saddle up, Lane."

"Can't go."

McKay looked at him as if he had not heard aright. A slight frown gathered between his brows. "You said you were not going?"

"That's right."

"But why?" McKay was incredulous.

"Gave my word I wouldn't."

"Your word? To whom?"

"Vittoro."

"Surely," Lieutenant McKay expostulated, "a word given to an Indian desperado can't be—"

"Lieutenant," Angie interrupted, "as an officer and a gentleman, surely you must agree that one's word given to anyone is binding."

"Of course." McKay flushed a little. "Sorry you must remind me, Mrs. Lowe. I forgot myself. Good day."

"Lieutenant," Hondo called after him, and the officer turned, "you won't have any trouble if you keep north of the butte. See it to the southwest about six miles out of here. You keep north.

Country south looks flat, but she's broken into canyons and washes."

"Thanks."

They stood together watching the Lieutenant walk away, carrying his back straight and walking as if on a drill field. The men were in the saddle, waiting. The sun was hot and the horses stamped restlessly, eager to be moving.

Lennie Sproul rode by, moving to his place near the head of the column. His jaw was badly swollen, his right eye closed. An ugly cut had opened his other cheekbone. He did not look at them as he passed, and when Buffalo Baker drew up near them he looked curiously at Hondo Lane.

"Lennie must've run into something," Buffalo commented, biting off a corner of his plug tobacco. "Had it comin', I reckon." He gathered his reins. "Wish you was with us, Hondo."

"Sorry."

Buffalo lifted a hand. "See you." He moved off to join Lieutenant McKay at the head of the column.

Then the column was moving, and the dust rose around them, then settled slowly, and the sun shone brightly on the last of the horses, glinted from the carbines. Neither of them moved.

Johnny walked down the trail of the horses and looked after them, his world suddenly empty with their going. He had never before seen so many soldiers, so many horses. He stood, scuffing his toe in the dirt, liking the smell of the horses, and remembering the easy, rough-handed friendship of the soldiers.

"Should have told you," Hondo said at last. "Tried to . . . didn't. It happened like this, Angie. I—"

She turned sharply away. "I can't talk now. I want to think. I need time. I'll put your war bag outside the cabin."

He watched her go, then walked to the corral. Uncertainly he looked around, trying to recall something he had intended doing, but the thought would not come. There was nothing in him, nothing but a vast impatience and a vast restlessness.

He looked up the trail the way the soldiers had gone, riding into battle. Because that was what it would be. Somewhere out there on some sun-blasted slope the Apaches would be waiting. Somewhere out there men would die.

Buffalo was along. . . . Luck to him, and to McKay and the others. That McKay, now, he was all right. Young, but he would grow into it. Proud, the way a young man should be, but conscious there was much to learn. He was the kind they needed out here. More officers like Crook, who understood the Indian.

Hearing the door open, he looked around. She was putting his war bag outside the door.

There it was, the end of whatever it had been, and all because of a small-caliber coyote who tried to shoot him in the back. He walked to the corral and led out the lineback. Then he went for his saddle.

TWENTY-ONE

The door slammed and Hondo glanced around. It was Johnny. Hands in pockets, the boy walked slowly toward him, looking big-eyed at the saddled horse.

"Goin' away?"

"Yeah."

"Can I come?"

"You better stay with your mother. She'll need you."

Johnny said nothing, kicking his toe into the dirt. He looked at the saddled horse with fear. Hondo Lane was going away, riding off without him.

"Nobody ever stays," he said.

Hondo glanced at him, packing his saddlebags. He checked the ammunition. Enough, but not too much. He refilled the empty loops in his belt, checked his gun and rifle.

"Pa rode off and never come back. Now you're ridin'."

Johnny watched him, fighting back tears.

Hondo turned his back. It was a lonely life for a kid. Only his mother here. The boy should have a father. He felt sick and miserable, thinking about that. This boy had no father, and it was his, Hondo's fault. But he had never had a father, actually.

167

Carrying his saddlebags to the lineback, he strapped them in place.

"You take care of your mother, you hear?"

"Yes," Johnny watched him, slowly drawing back. "You ain't comin' back." He said the words with sudden realization.

Hondo finished strapping the pack, then turned and, taking his time, began to build a smoke. He knew how the boy felt, because he had felt like that himself. When they were the age of this boy it was an awful thing to see a friend ride off. Later you became used to it. Later you learned that nothing was for long. It was a pity you had to learn that.

Hondo struck the match and lighted his cigarette. "Goin' to the fort. Maybe you'll come along someday. We'll have us a hunt together." He squatted on his heels. "You study sign, son. You remember what I taught you, an' try to learn more. Man walking in tall grass, he kicks the grass away from him in the direction he's travelin'. Horse or cow, their hoofs have a circular, swingin' motion, so they knock the grass down an' back. With them it points in the direction they come from."

Johnny had moved closer, but he did not look at Hondo. He stared at the ground, listening.

"No two animals and no two men leave the same track. Like signin' your name. Every one is different. You study at it, son. Readin' sign comes mighty handy."

He squeezed the boy's shoulder and got to his feet. His throat felt tight and choked up and he walked to his horse and gathered the reins. Then he put a hand on the pommel, and when he looked across the saddle, Angie was standing there, her face showing nothing. A tendril of hair hung down by one ear, stirring a little in the wind.

How white her shoulder was, where the dress pushed back from the tan! He felt himself tighten up inside, and then he said, "Didn't have any choice. He cut loose at me."

"I knew you were lying . . . to make me think well of him. Poor Ed. He wasn't the type of man to die well. I'm sorry now that I hated him so much . . . after I got to know how tawdry and weak he was. I guess he couldn't help being that way. He never saw the beauty of this country. Not the way my father and I saw it. He called it the country God forgot."

Hondo held the pommel, afraid to let go, afraid this little sign of hope would turn the fates against him. It was like keeping his fingers crossed.

"I didn't have a choice."

"I know."

He hesitated, waiting a long minute. "You going to feel different about me?"

"No one has any control about how they feel. I'm not going to change the way I feel about you."

Johnny had walked away, toward the stream. He did not want the man to go, but maybe his mother could do something about that. She always seemed able to do things about things.

"What about him?" Angie asked.

"What about him?" Hondo repeated the words thoughtfully. "Well, he'll make a man. Got a good spread to his shoulders. Head works, too. Tell him something, he remembers. Moves good—light on his feet. Other night while you were asleep he climbed on my bunk an' kissed me. Gave me a kind of funny feeling. First time I was ever kissed by a kid." Suddenly he dropped the reins to ground-hitch the lineback. "There's things I'd rather do than this."

Johnny was squatting near the river looking at some tracks, and Hondo walked slowly toward him.

Angie stared after him, feeling sudden panic as she realized what Hondo meant to do.

Johnny looked up from the tiny writing of tracks he had found. "Hondo, what track is that?"

Hondo squatted. "Squirrel there. This one with only four toes is the front foot. Back foot has five toes." He indicated another, larger track. "Badger. Follow him and you'll find holes where he dug out field mice or pack rats. He eats 'em. See the claw marks? Those are his front feet. Never see the claws on his back feet. Always toes in a mite, too."

Hondo rubbed his cigarette into the sand. "Want to tell you. While back a man came at me with a gun. Killed him."

"Good! Indian?"

"No. He was a white man. I didn't have any choice. This man I killed—"

"No!" Angie put her hand across his mouth. "Your ranch in California . . . California's far. Too far for gossip to travel."

Hondo got up slowly, relieved. Johnny wandered off, trailing the badger.

"California's far. He needs a father. He likes you, Hondo."

"Easy to say California's far, that he'll not hear. Could happen." He looked at her. "What then?"

"We'll face it then. Nobody lives their life without having to face things from time to time. It will work out, I know."

The cottonwood rustled its leaves and Hondo looked at the hills. She was right, of course. Face that issue when it came. By that time he would have been a father to the boy, and they would understand each other.

"The Apache don't have a word for love," he said. "Know what they both say at the marriage? The squaw-taking ceremony?"

"Tell me."

"*Varlebena*. It means forever. That's all they say."

Angie put her hand on his sleeve. "Forever," she said quietly. "Forever."

They stood together in silence, his arm about her waist. The lineback looked around impatiently, stomping a hoof at a fly. Johnny came trudging back from upstream. He looked at Hondo and his mother. "You going to stay?"

"Yes."

"Saw a hole that ol' badger dug."

He wandered off toward the corrals, and Angie looked up suddenly. "I'd hate to leave this place. Can the Lieutenant make us?"

"Guess so." They turned toward the house. "Better, anyway," he said. "No trouble around my place. Vittoro can't live forever."

"I planned to leave once, before you came back."

"Might have to. Anyway," he glanced around, "more grass

and trees on my place. When I left they talked some of building a school not far off. We got to think of that."

"All right."

She looked up at him. "Hondo, I . . . It's Father. He's buried back there in the trees. He—he liked the cottonwoods so much. I hate to leave him."

"You won't."

She looked up, and he said, "He left you. He lives in you and Johnny. I reckon no man ever dies who leaves a son or a daughter."

"We'll go, then?"

"We'll wait."

They heard the rush of hoofs and the rattle of wheels over stones before anything came into view, and then Johnny came running, and over the rim of the basin came a racing wagon. The horses lunged down the trail and drew up in a cloud of dust that overtook and settled around and over the wagon. Buffalo Baker was driving, and he sprang down and lifted the unconscious Lieutenant McKay from the wagon. The movement seemed to bring him out of it.

"We caught Vittoro," Buffalo said.

"Can't understand," McKay muttered, only half aware. "They had us surrounded. Could have cut us to pieces. Then they withdrew."

Hondo picked up a headband that had fallen from the wagon when the Lieutenant was lifted clear.

"Vittoro's."

"Killed him," Buffalo said, "on the last charge."

"Then that's it. That's why they pulled out. Any time the leader is killed, that means the medicine is bad."

He turned to Angie. "We'll go out with the squadron. Vittoro's dead."

Buffalo walked past them, carrying the Lieutenant through the door Angie held open.

"Now Silva's the leader. Get your things together."

"Wait. I've some medicines. Maybe I can do something for Lieutenant McKay."

"Thank you, Mrs. Lowe. I'd be grateful if you'd pass among the men and see what you can do for them."

"But you're bleeding, and—"

"Yes, ma'am, and many of the men are bleeding. I dislike to ask a lady to perform such a disagreeable task, but—"

When she had gone, McKay lay back on the bunk, breathing heavily. His eyes rolled toward Hondo. "You were right. Vittoro was just luring us on. Will you see that my troops get out."

He fainted then, and Hondo opened his shirt and went to work. He had that rough skill men acquired on a frontier where doctors were rare, and medicines even rarer.

"He didn't know much," Buffalo said. "He led us into an ambush. But I ain't ashamed of him, nohow. All his bullet holes is in the front part of him."

Hondo had taken warm water from the stove and was gently sponging away the blood from the wounds. "All them youngsters from West Point is like that."

"They got to learn."

"Partly they learn, partly they die. I got to float my stick same as you. I never saw one of them I had to be ashamed of."

He worked on, sponging off the wounds, then binding them with Indian remedies. They were methods he had used on himself, and they worked.

Finally he straightened up. "Better get them started out there. Take the wagon here, harness the horses, and load the wounded. There's a good deal of bedding. We won't have much time."

"You think Silva will come here?"

"Yes." Hondo Lane turned and glanced out the door to Angie, coming toward the house. "It'll be first on his list."

TWENTY-TWO

Westward the land was bright. The moving column wound like a gray-blue snake across the beige-gray hills. Sweat streaked the faces of the troopers and dust settled on the blue of their uniforms. Many were stained with the blood of their enemies, and not a few with the blood of their own veins. The wagons rolled and rumbled, jolting over the stones, and in one of the wagons a man cursed in a high, hard, monotonous voice.

Saddles creaked; men watched the hills. Sweat darkened the hides of the horses. The sun was hot. The uniforms of the men were stiff with ancient sweat and dust, and their lips cracked. Occasionally a low wind moved among them, cooling and fresh like a draught of cold clear water.

Sergeant Young mopped his face and looked over at Hondo. "You think he's coming?"

"I know he is."

"How much time we got?"

"Three-four hours."

"Wished the Lieutenant was up."

Hondo Lane said nothing. He knew how the Sergeant felt. They were pitifully short of officers all along the frontier.

Lane dropped back along the column, then swept the hills

173

behind them. No sign of anything yet, but it was too soon. But once the medicine was made, Silva would not wait long. He was dangerous, but too impatient. He would be relentless and ruthless, but less shrewd than old Vittoro had been.

Behind the column the dust settled and there were only the tracks, a plain trail that nothing could remove. Not even a bad storm would wipe out that trail, and behind them would be the Mescaleros and their allies.

He looked around at the parched and lonely country, then swung the lineback. There was yet time, but to hole up and make a stand would be worse than useless. They must keep going, get near enough for a relief column to reach them.

He rode after the moving train, and they plodded on wearily, pushing toward the afternoon and the rim of distant hills beyond the post, still so far, far away.

There was a brief noon halt near a water hole whose waters swiftly dwindled and died as the horses drank. No man touched any water but that from his canteen, and sparingly. The horses were all-important now, and each horse drank.

Lieutenant McKay was delirious, talking of Richmond, of the Point, and of a girl somewhere who had said no, when she could not have found a better man.

The sun was high and hot. Fifteen minutes of halt, then the column moved out. Men slumped in the saddle, weary after miles, yet knowing what was yet to come. In the wagons the cursing man had lost consciousness, and a man with a broken collarbone and a bandaged skull was singing to a mandolin the good songs, the old songs. . . .

In the hot stillness of the afternoon they came down from the hills, their dark bodies dusty with the trail and the column swung its few wagons into a tight circle and the rifles spoke. The Indians vanished, then came again, swiftly, some on horseback, but more upon foot. The Apache was a daring runner, and he trusted his feet.

Cold eyes looked down the barrels of rifles and then men fired. Dust leaped from the hillside. An Apache stopped in mid-stride as though he had run headlong into some obstruction, and then he fell, his shrill dying cry hanging in the stillness of the afternoon long after the man was dead.

The charge ended, the rush was gone, the hillside was a barren and empty thing, alive with death.

Like ghosts, somebody said. Vanished, melted into the landscape, as was the Apache way. A rifle spoke. A trooper cried out and died. Hondo rode swiftly around the inner circle. He called his orders in a low, hard voice, Sergeant Young making the other loop. The rush came suddenly, and as it did the column sprang into life and went hurtling forward, wagons three abreast, horses racing, surrounded by cavalry.

It caught the Apaches by surprise. Most of them were dismounted, moving forward among the rocks. It caught them unprepared and the tight knot of wagons and men rolled out and over the crest and down the long sweep of the valley. A mile fell behind . . . two miles. Whooping Indians came up behind, firing and missing, yet racing forward.

Hondo yelled at Young and the Sergeant gave a quick command. Ten troopers swung their horses into line and dropped to the ground, to their knees. An instant they waited as the Apaches charged nearer. The volley was a solid sound, a sound that struck and melted the advancing Indians. Swiftly the kneeling men fired again.

Leaving chaos behind them, they swung into their saddles and were off after the train.

"We'll try that again!" Young yelled.

"Won't work again," Hondo said. "They'll be scattered out now."

But some of the attackers had gone on ahead, cutting across the hills, and now they came down, pouring over the crest like a dark flood, lit by flashes of color and flame. The wagons rounded again into a circle and the troopers swung down from their horses. Hondo put the butt of his Winchester against his shoulder and fired, his shots seeking out the Apaches, firing carefully, squeezing off every shot.

Attacks began and ended. The Apache was never one to trust a wild charge. He was a shrewd and careful fighter, knowing the value of cover, moving with care, never wasting time or shots. They moved in closer, then closer.

They were elusive, targets scarcely seen. A flash of brown against the desert, then no sign of life, no movement. Worming their way closer, they used scant inches of cover for their movements. When they came again it would be from close up, their charge only a few yards. Hondo worked his way around, warning the troopers to be ready. He scattered the few men with pistols in positions to cover every yard of space.

A half hour passed. The sun beat down from a wide and brassy sky. Sweat trickled down the faces and necks of the waiting troopers. Its salt made them blink. Their rifles were hot from the desert sun.

The Apaches knew the value of waiting, and as they waited, they drew nearer. A single rifle shot sounded. A trooper had seen a flashing brown leg and fired. His shot ripped the heel from the vanishing Indian.

Silence lay heavily upon the circle. Heat waves shimmered. A man coughed, a horse stamped at a fly. There was no other sound. Hondo shifted his Colt, drying a sweaty palm. They waited, hugging their sparse cover.

Suddenly fifty horsemen charged over the hill. Eyes lifted to them and rifles . . . and in that instant, the nearer Indians charged also. It was perfect—except for Hondo's pistol men.

There were six of them in all, but their fire was point-blank. It broke the force of the charge, and the Indians that reached the barricades were clubbed down by battering rifle butts. And then the horsemen came.

Some had gone down, but a dozen leaped their horses into the circle. One big brave lunged his horse at Hondo, his lance poised. Hondo's side step saved him and his quick grasp of the lance wrenched the Indian from the saddle. The Indian hit on the small of his neck, and as he tried to roll over, Hondo kicked him under the chin, then shot him.

A horse was down, screaming. The inner circle was a whirl of fighting men. From the outer circle came the heavy bark of rifles to prove that Indians were still coming. Lieutenant McKay was on one elbow, firing his pistol.

Hondo swung his pistol barrel at a head, heard it crunch, saw a lance aimed for him and swung aside. And then in the swirl of dust and smoke he saw Silva.

The big Indian's face was a twisted mask of fury and he leaped his horse at Hondo. The animal's shoulder hit Hondo and he was knocked rolling. Silva swung down from his horse and sprang, knife in hand. Hondo came up from the ground and his kick caught Silva below the knee. The Indian stopped in mid-stride and another Apache swept by. Hondo struck out at him and saw the man fall, then caught up his broken lance in time to meet Silva's lance. He parried the blow, then gutted the Indian as the Indian had gutted the dog.

Silva went down, the lance ripping him up, and Hondo said, "Like my dog . . . you die!"

As suddenly as it had begun, the attack broke. A swarm of Apaches swept round him, and then they were gone, carrying Silva among them.

And then there was only settling dust and the moans of the wounded and the dying.

Again the wagons rolled, only now there were more wounded, now there were empty saddles, now there were more bandaged heads.

Sergeant Young dropped back beside the wagon where Hondo rode. "That hurt 'em!" he said. "We hurt 'em bad!"

"They won't bother us."

"You don't think they'll attack again?"

"Another chief's dead. We'll make the fort before they have another leader."

Angie started to bandage a wound on Hondo's arm. He handed the reins to Johnny, who accepted them eagerly.

"He's never learned to drive!" Angie protested.

"By the time we make California, he'll be top teamster." He yelled shrilly at the horses, and they moved out.

Angie finished with the arm, and held it, and all up and down the column there was only the movement of wagons rolling, the sound of horses' hoofs, and an occasional low moan from a wagon.

From far back in the column a mandolin sounded and a rolling bass started the words of "Sweet Betsy from Pike."

A long time later, when the column rolled over the long hill and headed for the parade ground, Hondo looked up from the reins he now held. He could see the flag fluttering in the wind, the troops marching onto the field for retreat, and westward the land was bright with a setting sun, and a dull rose shaded the clouds and faded away against the higher heavens, and from the parade ground he heard a bugle, its notes bright and clear.

He heard Sergeant Young's command, saw the men form up, and saw them, battered and wounded and bloody, riding proudly to the parade ground.

He saw them go, and knew their fierce pride, and their glory. But he was remembering a long meadow fresh with new-cut hay, a house where smoke would soon again rise from the chimney, and where shadows would gather in the darkness under the trees, quiet shadows. And beside him a woman held in her arms a sleeping child . . . a woman who would be there with him, in that house, before that hearth.